Buddy's eyes were closed and his head thrown back, the water gently falling first on his head and then slowly down his body. Every drop took away more grime and dirt, washing away some of the accumulated bad things that had happened to him over the last week—or however long it had been. Maybe, just maybe, if he scrubbed away enough, he might even find out who he was. Between the wonderful feel of the shower and the thought of learning his identity, Buddy had to smile.

If Jack had been transfixed before, now the guy was wet, hunky, and happy, Jack was a goner. He sighed. This mystery man was absolutely gorgeous.

Welcome to
Dreamspun Desires

Dear Reader,

Love is the dream. It dazzles us, makes us stronger, and brings us to our knees. Dreamspun Desires tell stories of love featuring your favorite heartwarming heroes, captivating plots, and exotic locations. Stories that make your breath catch and your imagination soar.

In the pages of these wonderful love stories, readers can escape to a world where love conquers all, the tenderness of a first kiss sweeps you away, and your heart pounds at the sight of the one you love.

When you put it all together, you find romance in its truest form.

Love always finds a way.

Elizabeth North

Executive Director
Dreamspinner Press

Michael Murphy

STRANGER IN A
FOREIGN LAND

PUBLISHED BY

Published by
DREAMSPINNER PRESS

5032 Capital Circle SW, Suite 2, PMB# 279,
Tallahassee, FL 32305-7886 USA
www.dreamspinnerpress.com

This is a work of fiction. Names, characters, places, and incidents either are the product of author imagination or are used fictitiously, and any resemblance to actual persons, living or dead, business establishments, events, or locales is entirely coincidental.

Stranger in a Foreign Land
© 2018 Michael Murphy.

Cover Art
© 2018 Bree Archer.
http://www.breearcher.com
Cover content is for illustrative purposes only and any person depicted on the cover is a model.

Paperback ISBN: 978-1-64108-048-4
Digital ISBN: 978-1-64080-250-6
Library of Congress Control Number: 2017916040
Paperback published July 2018
v. 1.0

Printed in the United States of America
∞
This paper meets the requirements of
ANSI/NISO Z39.48-1992 (Permanence of Paper).

Originally from rural upstate New York, **MICHAEL MURPHY** grew up walking through fields of corn taller than most people, riding horses, and driving on dirt roads. For more than thirty years, he has lived in Washington, DC, where there aren't many dirt roads or horses.

His biggest influences when growing up were his two grandmothers. Both were ferociously strong women who were widowed young while they still had children at home. Neither remarried, but they picked up the shattered pieces of their lives and built new lives for themselves. They taught him that the underdog could come out on top if he or she just tried.

Those women loved to read and to tell stories, so it just always seemed a natural thing for him to want to do the same. When he hit a major milestone birthday, he realized that there were fewer years left in which to do things than there had already been. He made a bucket list, which had writing a book at the top of the list. With his twentieth book now in the editorial production process, that dream has been realized and has been one of the highlights of his life.

Visit his website at www.gayromancewriter.com to learn more about him and his writing.

This one is for Danny,
who shared that first trip to Thailand with me
many years ago, where this story was born.

Chapter One
Welcome to Thailand

THE wheels of the fully loaded 747 jumbo jet slammed down onto the runway in Bangkok, as rough a landing as the flight had been. Despite the jarring touchdown, Patrick had a sense of overwhelming joy for the fact that this leg of his trip was nearly over. Perhaps it would be more appropriate to say he felt the anticipation of impending great joy, because otherwise he felt like day-old dog crap.

Every time Patrick made this flight, he told himself he would never again subject himself to the ordeal. Surely he would remember before agreeing to another such trip that flights that lasted more than twelve hours were killers. But every time, he forgot and agreed once again to make the long haul halfway around the world.

This time—with God as his witness—*this time* would be different, he told himself, as the plane that had moments before so gracefully glided through the air, now lumbered across the taxiway, swaying as it made its way slowly to the terminal.

This trip had included the added misery because he'd waited too late to book his ticket. His work in London had taken longer than originally budgeted, so he'd had to postpone his departure for Bangkok. When he'd finally been able to leave London, all the first-class and business-class seats for the flight from London to Bangkok were gone. Although he wanted to pay to sit up front with more room so he could work—maybe lie back and sleep for a while—he was relegated to the back of the bus with the rest of the passengers in coach. If he hadn't been so pressed for time, he would have waited and taken another flight, one where he could have gotten a seat in first class. But he was due in a meeting first thing the next morning, so flexibility and time were two luxuries he did not have on this leg of the trip. He'd had to suck it up and deal with the situation, but that didn't stop him from grumbling to himself.

When they had finally parked at the gate, he knew no matter how much he wanted to be off that airplane—and he really, really, really wanted to get off—it would only further the torture to even think about getting out of his seat just yet. Nothing was going to happen right away; no one was going to move anytime soon where he was seated near the back of the plane, so why bother even trying. Standing would only take him from his uncomfortable seat to stand uncomfortably in the overcrowded aisle, assuming he could even squeeze into it.

He had read the reports by the so-called experts on how a fully loaded 747 could be evacuated in something like ninety seconds. He wondered why those same experts didn't make a report on how long it took to deplane a fully loaded 747 after a twelve-hour flight, when everyone had to get out of their seat, stretch their sore and aching muscles, find their carry-ons, hit someone by accident with luggage that was too large, then have to stop and hold up everyone else while they apologized, and finally make their way off the plane. Deplaning was not a speedy process, especially when one was seated way, way in the back as Patrick was on this flight.

As he waited, he was neither patient nor impatient. He was just sort of numb. When the hordes of humanity closest to him finally started to move, Patrick tried to remember how his legs worked. After collecting his briefcase from under the seat in front of him, he crawled out of his godforsaken middle seat at the back of the coach cabin, grabbed his one small carry-on bag, and then started to move with the herd off the plane.

When the air on the jet bridge touched his face, it felt like someone had thrown a hot, wet, smelly blanket over his head. Ah, yes, a cool day in Bangkok.

He knew that after drinking about a gallon of water, spending about an hour in the shower, followed by ten hours of sleep, then and only then would he start to feel like a real human being again. But he couldn't let his mind go there just yet. No. There were too many hurdles to get through between where he was and those good feelings.

The walkway from the airplane into the terminal always reminded him of the chutes cattle were forced into on their way to the slaughterhouse. He didn't know what had originally placed that image into his head, but once there, it would not leave. Now, every time he found himself walking through one of the things, that vision came rushing back to him uninvited.

Patrick had made his first trip to Thailand many years earlier, when flights came into an older airport in a different part of town. For the last several years, all flights arrived at the still relatively new airport. The only problem was the new airport had a lot more capacity, and more capacity brought more planes, which brought more people, which made for a bit of chaos at times getting out of the airport.

In addition to being a ridiculously long flight, this flight had been especially torturous because of bad weather. Huge storms somewhere over Belarus or Kazakhstan had woken up most of the people who had settled in to try to get some sleep. There was something about getting tossed around on a darkened plane in the middle of the night that was especially frightening, even for a road warrior like Patrick.

The flight had left London's Heathrow Airport pretty much on time a few minutes after ten o'clock on Saturday night. Patrick had hoped to get some sleep, but the experience of filling the plane to capacity and then shaking it vigorously for roughly one-quarter of the distance did not lend itself to rest.

Their pilot had dutifully tried to find better conditions by detouring around the worst of the weather, but in the end, there was only so much he could do.

Patrick had not been able to get much sleep, so with nothing else to do, he had sat in his middle seat and watched the little airplane symbol on the map on the seatback in front of him as it slowly—ever so slowly—inched its way across Belarus, Kazakhstan, Kyrgyzstan, China, a sliver of Nepal, and finally, finally over Myanmar before they started their descent into Bangkok, Thailand, where they landed at about three thirty Sunday afternoon. With the time change of six hours and the flight time of twelve, it was only eighteen hours, but to Patrick and everyone else who crawled off the plane that hot, muggy afternoon, it felt like a lifetime had passed since they boarded.

For once, the lines at the various checkpoints were not too ridiculous. Still, Patrick unfailingly picked one of the slower lines, then inched his way through, showing his passport when required, turning in documents he'd completed aboard the plane, and answering questions asked of him.

When he finally had his suitcase in hand and had cleared every checkpoint, he strode through the terminal. The last hurdle was another line, this one for a cab to take him into the city to his hotel. At least inside the airport when he'd stood in line, it had been air-conditioned. But the cab line was outside in the lingering heat and overwhelming humidity of an afternoon in Thailand.

The line moved slowly, with there being more passengers than cabs, for some reason. He didn't know if it was the convergence of multiple jumbo jets arriving at the same time, but the cab line was interminable. Patrick was exhausted, and the longer he waited, the more he sweat and the more uncomfortable he became. Finally the line moved, and it was his turn.

After the driver had stashed his suitcase in the trunk of the cab, Patrick crawled into the back seat of the small Thai car and closed his eyes for a few minutes. He tried picturing the welcoming grand lobby of his hotel, a place he'd stayed many times and knew rather well. Without intending to do so, he drifted to sleep for a few minutes.

He opened his eyes blearily and looked around. Was he at his hotel already? No. But something had woken him. What the hell was it? Ah. He saw now that his cabdriver was trying to hand him something. Hadn't he seen Patrick sleeping? Tipping didn't mean the same thing in Thailand, so Patrick wouldn't be able to undertip to express his dissatisfaction.

When he had roused himself enough to figure out who he was and where he was, Patrick instinctively reached out and took what the driver was trying to shove his way. One glance, though, told him all he needed to know. The driver was attempting to persuade him to rent a prostitute from him. Patrick didn't know if the woman was supposed to be the driver's wife or sister or mother or some random stranger. He didn't care. He didn't go for women and certainly wouldn't willingly sleep with some stranger a cabdriver in a foreign land was pushing on him.

The driver was half turned around, smiling at Patrick. He seemed extraordinarily eager for Patrick to look at the photos, as if looking at them would change his mind. His English was horrible, but Patrick knew what the guy was doing and didn't want to play that game. He shook his head and shoved the plastic-covered photos back to the man. The driver smiled more and gestured for Patrick to look some more. Patrick caught something about "good deal." When the guy wouldn't take the pictures back, Patrick simply dropped them onto the front seat beside the driver.

Thai people can be very gentle, quiet people, but this driver was neither. He wanted to make a sale and was not pleased Patrick wasn't interested. He was turning back toward Patrick to say something. Patrick was looking at him, dreading the idea of a dispute with a non-English-speaking cabdriver in a foreign country.

But neither of them needed to worry, at least about that. While the driver had been distracted trying to convince Patrick of the great deal he had for him, their car had veered slightly across the lines separating the two lanes of traffic. Before a single word of argument could be uttered, a truck slammed into the front of the driver's side of the cab with a vicious force, not only stopping their forward momentum but also snapping the car hard as they spun out of control. It all happened so fast the collision pushed the car into the path of another vehicle, which smashed into the front end of the other side of the cab, whipping them around.

Another truck smashed into the second car, which crushed some more of the cab. The third collision somehow loosened the cab from the other vehicles, and it slid sideways over the edge of the road and down a concrete embankment. The angle of descent was enough that the cab started to roll and did three complete rotations before coming to rest upside down in a crumpled heap of twisted metal and plastic.

It was irrelevant to the driver—he'd died almost instantly when the first truck hit the vehicle. But it was very much relevant for Patrick in the back seat, or more properly what was left of the back seat, which now sat where part of the trunk had once rested. Most of the trunk had been sheared off at one stage or another of the various encounters with other vehicles.

No one could come through a massive traumatic crash like that one and walk away without a scratch. Patrick was indeed scratched and scraped, bumped and bruised, and even burned in one place. He'd been thrown around the inside of the cab from one side to the other and back again before the small car had taken its final roll down the embankment. He barely realized it, but his left shoulder was injured and would soon hurt like crazy.

During their crash, Patrick's head had banged hard into the window, or something else in the car. Even though the cab was no longer moving, he was having a miserable time trying to stop the world from spinning.

Any fatigue Patrick had felt was automatically erased by the adrenaline flooding his bloodstream. As that rush of hormones subsided a bit, Patrick felt an overwhelming urge to simply lie back now that his world had stopped flipping end over end. Blood dripped over one eye from a horrible cut on his forehead. He felt woozy and just wanted to be still for a moment. Whether he was conscious or not didn't matter; he just wanted his world to stabilize.

But he wasn't given that choice. A spark from somewhere ignited the gasoline leaking from the car. Patrick was close enough to both the gas and the fire that his primitive fight-or-flight instinct kicked in. He knew without thinking that fire meant danger and he had to get the hell out of there. His bleeding forehead and the dizziness made it difficult for him to see straight, but he managed to feel his way to an opening of some sort. He didn't know exactly what, nor did it really matter.

As he pulled himself through the opening in the twisted carcass of the vehicle, one leg of his suit pants caught on a jagged piece of metal and tore half of that piece of cloth away. His jacket fared no better. He caught the left sleeve on another piece of metal and left it behind as he struggled to get free. He smelled the smoke and felt the heat of the flames, so he knew getting out, getting away, was all that mattered if he wanted to live for more than the next sixty seconds.

Before Patrick departed from home, first for London and then for Bangkok, he had purchased sufficient British pounds for the first part of his trip and

Thai baht for the second. But all his currency was either in the inside pocket of his jacket, in his wallet (which was in his briefcase, which was still inside the cab), or in the pocket of his pants—the pants that had been torn as he crawled from the cab. But none of that mattered to Patrick at the moment. In fact, none of those thoughts were anywhere near the front of his mind. First and foremost was the basic instinct to survive.

When he pulled himself clear of the crumpled cab, he stayed down and just kept scrambling, intent on putting distance between himself and the mangled wreck.

He hadn't gotten ten feet before a massive explosion ripped through the air. Patrick instinctively threw himself flat onto the concrete, assuming it was his cab that had just blown up. It took him nearly thirty seconds to realize the explosion had come from somewhere else. Looking around he saw his cab still burning and still too close, so he got back onto his hands and knees and kept crawling away.

After he had covered about fifty feet, he ran out of space to move because the concrete platform ended and he could see the river below. But that didn't matter because Patrick's attention was ripped away by the sound of his cab exploding. The combination of fire and gasoline had produced the cataclysmic reaction he'd instinctively feared.

When the first explosion had happened, Patrick had dropped to the ground. He didn't get a choice on this one—the force of the blast knocked him down.

Patrick rolled over onto his back as the fireball of flames engulfed the cab. Pieces of the vehicle blown away by the explosion started to rain down. Instinctively he rolled to his side and attempted to curl into a fetal position so he could shield his body the best he could from the pieces of hot or burning metal and plastic. The blast of heat from the explosion threatened to push him over the edge and into the river below.

Once the initial roar of the flames died back, Patrick knew he had to get the hell out of there. The heat of the flames was licking at him. He had to put some distance between the burning cab and himself.

With the river to one side, flames from the road on the other, and his own burning cab behind him, he fled the only way left open to him. He simply focused on moving away from the heat of the fire. It took some work, but he managed to stand up and walk and to eventually climb out of the concrete valley he was in. He walked a fair distance before he found a spot with a less steep incline that allowed him to climb up, and eventually he made it up to road level.

When he got to the road level, he looked left and then right, but nothing seemed familiar. He didn't know where he was or which way he should go.

At the very moment Patrick came closest to flat-out screaming panic, he realized not only did he not know where he was, but he also did not know *who* he was. He was no longer Patrick. He was a stranger in a very foreign land, a man with absolutely no clue about anything.

Chapter Two
What Once Was Found
Has Now Been Lost

THE man looked at his surroundings yet again, hoping something would strike him as familiar. The highway he'd been on was empty, due to the accident he'd been part of. But just ahead, his highway merged with another one filled with traffic. He stood unsteadily for a moment, studying the traffic, but none of the cars looked familiar. Even the sounds of the cars and the trucks near his location were foreign to his ear.

Spotting the back of what looked like a street sign, he hobbled forward, hoping it would be the source of some information. But those hopes were dashed when he finally reached the sign. All he saw were curly white markings on a green background. He supposed those markings could be letters, most likely making up words, but it was all academic because none of them made any sense to him. Were they names of streets? Of towns? Cities? He didn't have a clue. And it didn't answer the question he had foremost on his mind: where the fuck was he?

He wished his head would stop hurting. Every step he took amplified the pain. When he closed his eyes for a moment, the pain seemed to lessen. But he didn't really feel he could stop just then, not without figuring out who he was and where he was.

Hoping that if he moved to a different area he might find something familiar, he started walking in the direction he'd walked in to get to the street sign. Even though every step made him grimace, for twenty minutes he trudged along, every few minutes stopping to check for anything he might recognize. But there was nothing. Just more of the same small cars racing past him on a road he didn't know.

What he did recognize, though, was feeling absolutely wiped out, exhausted like he'd just run a marathon. He didn't think he'd run a race, given the way he was dressed—or rather, what was left of how he had been dressed.

When the highway along which he was walking branched, he followed the one that appeared to lead into a quieter street, or at least a less traveled street. He opted for that and hobbled down the exit ramp to the smaller surface road. Once he was on the street, he realized it was filled with warehouses, and they all looked dark and empty.

He trudged on, and time lost all meaning as he wandered up one street and down another. Even as the afternoon gave way to evening and it grew dark as night fell, the air was just so damned hot and humid. When the pain in his head and his fatigue simply became too much, he found a dark spot, lay down, and quickly fell asleep.

WHEN he stirred awake sometime later, night was gone, replaced by a blazing-hot day. Looking around, he couldn't entirely remember which direction he'd been headed, so he picked one at random and hobbled off that way. He was astonished at how little traffic he encountered where he was walking. The part of town he found himself in had seen better days, days when it had filled some role. Now it looked desolate and deserted.

The day was swelteringly hot and humid, and he was perspiring profusely. He wanted nothing more than to sit in the shade and have a cold drink of water. When he spotted a quiet, shady place a little way off the street, he headed toward that spot. While he found the shade he craved, it unfortunately didn't have any source of water. Still, he took a break from walking and sat down.

Sitting on the concrete in the shade offered little relief, and he could feel the heat radiating up into his body. He decided after only a couple of minutes that the heat from the concrete was just as bad as walking, so he hoisted himself back to his feet and trudged onward, looking for something better.

The heat and humidity were taking their toll on him. He staggered a bit, like someone who had had too much to drink, when exactly the opposite was the case. He was becoming dehydrated and overheated. He desperately needed a rest, some water, and someplace to cool off.

He didn't know where he was going to find what he needed, but his body didn't give him a choice in the matter. When he collapsed to the ground, the decision was made for him. The only fortunate thing was he fell into a shady spot and in such a manner he didn't hurt himself further.

He was only unconscious for a few minutes. He would have remained unconscious longer if a passing shower had not moved into his area and drenched him and everything around him. All the shower did for the air was fill it with even more moisture, if that was possible. He hadn't believed anything could be more humid than the air he'd been walking in, but he was proven wrong.

The rain, such as it was, brought him back to consciousness. Momentarily confused about where he was, he had a bit of a panic attack when he couldn't figure out who he was or why he was there.

When he was more fully conscious, he remembered he hadn't known who he was before passing out. The only good thing was he realized he was terribly thirsty and the sudden rain shower had helped with the thirst problem. He didn't have a cup or a bowl or anything to catch the water as it fell from the sky, so he did the next best thing and used his hands to catch some of the rain pouring down from above. His hands were inefficient for catching rainwater, but each time he had some water he raised his hands to his mouth and gratefully drank. It would have been wonderful if the water had been cold, but given the heat of the day, even warm water was welcome at that point.

The shower finished just as quickly as it had arrived. The rain had felt wonderful while falling, but when the sun reappeared a few moments later, the moisture in the air became even more stifling than before. The heat and humidity of the area were absolutely debilitating.

He thought the best thing to do was to find a quiet place in the shade and try to rest for a few minutes in the hopes he might be able to remember who he was and where he was. He spotted a quiet, out-of-the-way corner in a shady spot and fell to the ground. Less than sixty seconds later, he was asleep.

WHEN he woke, it was dark once again. The heat had not diminished much, but at least the sun was no longer baking everything it touched. He looked around from where he lay, in the hopes he would spot something familiar and he would suddenly know the answers to all the questions swirling in his mind.

Unfortunately that was not the case. The area was now as dark as it had been bright earlier in the day, and he couldn't see anything or tell anything about where he was. He could hear traffic moving nearby on what sounded like a highway, but he couldn't see the traffic.

Not sure whether he should try to get up and explore in the hopes of finding some answers, or simply lie where he was and get more rest, the decision was made for him when he fell back to sleep. When next he was aware of anything, he felt two overwhelming urges—he needed to pee and he was hungry.

As he stood to relieve himself, he noticed the hint of morning light in the sky. As he peed against a brick wall near where he'd slept, he looked around, but nothing was familiar.

Issue one resolved, he turned his attention to issue number two. As if to reinforce the decision, he felt his stomach rumble and growl. He couldn't remember the last time he had eaten. Since he couldn't remember anything else, he might have eaten a fantastic meal recently and just not remembered it. His stomach disagreed.

He didn't know his own name or anything about himself. He also didn't know where he normally got food. His hunger drove him to the only alternative he could identify; it was time to go scavenging for food. Maybe, if he was lucky, he might find some answers along with something to eat.

Chapter Three
Hunger, Pain, and Fear

ONE of the few constants he had was the never-ending noise of the distant traffic—the hum of car and truck tires on a hot road. He knew the traffic was from a highway, and it would be difficult to walk across a highway.

As he walked away from the highway noise in search of food, he shoved his hands into his pockets— nothing there. He had no identification and, more importantly at that moment, no money. Maybe he'd never had money. Maybe he was a bum who just lived on the streets, homeless and destitute.

He staggered a little, because when he'd woken that morning, his body was very, very sore and movement was difficult. He had pain in a variety of places. He couldn't imagine why he hurt so much. His only guess was he'd been involved in some sort of altercation and he'd been injured.

For about half an hour, he wandered throughout the warehouse district, desperate to find something to eat. He checked several dumpsters, hoping one of the warehouses might be a food distribution one, but each time his search was without success. He found more cardboard and nonedible things than he could believe, but no food.

His hunger continued to gnaw at him, seemingly trying to eat away at his very body from the stomach out. After nearly forty-five minutes of walking—or wandering—he spotted something completely out of place. He wasn't sure what it was at first, but it was different enough to make him walk toward it to check it out.

When he got close enough, he could see it was a small ramshackle house—a shack, more accurately. And there wasn't just one. From what he could tell, there were several similar shacks in a row. They looked like a good wind would take them down, but surprisingly the area all around them was immaculate. Even more surprising, when he studied the situation a bit more carefully, there were flowers planted in front of the one that had first caught his attention. Flowers? He didn't understand it, but he was too hungry to give it any further thought.

The plants around the shack were not just flowers. In the *front yard*, for lack of any better term, there were plants with what looked like edible things. He saw some tomatoes, a couple of pineapple plants, and a bunch of other things he couldn't readily identify.

He didn't know who he was, but he knew taking something from someone else was wrong. He hated even considering it, but he was so very hungry... and scared. Before he could think of any other reasons why he shouldn't do it, he raced to the closest tomato plant and plucked off the largest ripest-looking tomato. He immediately took a big bite out of the fruit.

Why did he know a tomato was a fruit and not a vegetable? He felt a pain in his head that made him nearly drop what was left of the tomato. Had he been able to slow down and savor the taste, he would have realized the tomato he was eating was one of the best he'd ever tasted. Of course, to make that evaluation, he would have needed to remember eating other tomatoes to have some points of reference.

At that moment, all he knew was he was hungry and he was eating something to make his hunger less of an issue. He finished the first tomato and was reaching for another when he heard something that startled him. Quickly he looked up to identify the noise. And he found it. Standing about ten feet away from him was an older woman—small, Asian, and clearly pissed off with him.

Like a deer in headlights, he was frozen for a few seconds. The woman was not frozen. He couldn't understand a single word she said, but she said them with tremendous energy and conviction. Even though he couldn't identify the words she used, he could clearly hear the scolding in her voice. And if he hadn't noticed that, the look on her face would have conveyed the same message. In her eyes he had done something wrong, something extremely bad, and she wasn't about to let it pass without comment.

Thinking quickly, he could only guess it was because the tomatoes in question belonged to her. He didn't want a confrontation with an angry little woman, so he quickly reached down and grabbed the tomato he'd been after.

With the fruit in hand, he turned and started to run away from the scary little woman. He had just turned around when he felt something hit him on his upper back. Whatever had collided with his body carried enough force to throw off his center of gravity, and he tumbled flat onto the hard blacktop, dropping the tomato.

Slightly confused, he looked around to see what had hit him and spotted a large pineapple. Clearly the old lady had thrown whatever was close at hand. Since she was still yelling—something—at him, he quickly shook off his momentary confusion, grabbed the pineapple, and got back on his feet, all to get the hell away from the old woman with the killer pitching arm.

The pineapple had hit him with enough force to knock him over, but it was only when he was back on his feet and running once again that he noticed the heavy piece of fruit had impacted him enough to really hurt. He tried to ignore the pain in his upper back. After all, the rest of his body was already in pain, so this new one had plenty of company.

Between the stifling heat, the wet blanket of humidity—oh, and getting coldcocked by a five-pound pineapple—he didn't feel up to a long run. He rounded the corner of the building where he'd slept the previous night and dropped into the first shaded spot he found.

Had he stuck around for thirty seconds longer, he would have been able to see the old lady's neighbors all appear at the sound of the commotion.

MOST of the folks who lived in the little collection of ramshackle huts were Thai natives, like the old lady,

Boon Tan. But one was not. One, a relative newcomer in that he'd only been with them for a couple of years, was a native of Australia. Where the Thai folks were smaller and a bit darker in complexion, the man from Australia was tall, white, and blond. He looked more like a beach bum or a surfer dude than anything else. Of course he'd come running, wearing only a pair of shorts, when he heard Boon Tan yelling so loudly and angrily.

While not a native, Jack Rupert spoke impeccable Thai, in addition to the Queen's English. He wasted no time in asking Boon Tan what was wrong.

"Crazy-looking man scared me. I came out and he was eating my tomatoes."

"What did he look like?" Jack asked her.

"Like you."

"Like me how?"

"Not Thai. Tall. Light skin. Only this one looked strange."

"Strange how?"

"His clothes were all wrong. That's what scared me so much at first. He was wearing what looked like it had been a nice suit at one time. Only the jacket was torn in half, the pants were all ripped, and it looked like he'd rolled around in dirt and mud and oil. And he had blood all over his face and the one bare arm."

"He was bleeding?"

"No. I said he had blood. If I'd meant he was bleeding, I would have said he was bleeding. The blood was dried, so he'd been bleeding recently but not too recently."

"He took off when he saw you?" Jack asked, trying to get the rest of the story.

"Yes. But I was scared, so I threw a pineapple at him—knocked him off his feet and stunned him. I hope

I didn't hurt him too bad," she said, holding her hand in front of her mouth, suddenly concerned she'd done the wrong thing.

"Which way did he go?" Jack asked.

She pointed in the direction she'd seen the strange man run. Jack wished he had his shoes on, but he didn't want to waste the time it would take to go back to his house and grab them, so he took off barefoot. One step onto the hot blacktop was almost enough to make him change his mind, but he decided to simply run fast and try to ignore the pain.

He rounded the building where Boon Tan had last seen the stranger, fully expecting him to be long gone. He was therefore surprised to easily spot the man huddled beside a trash dumpster. Boon Tan had been right—he was a mess. Every single point she'd described had been accurate. Blood. Torn clothes. Grimy. And white. The guy most certainly wasn't Thai or Southeast Asian.

Standing barefoot on the hot blacktop was not an option, so Jack quickly and quietly advanced on the man, trying to not make him bolt. He needn't have worried, though. The guy was totally involved in trying to smash open the pineapple in his hand. When he succeeded in breaking the fruit into two pieces, he took careful bites.

The pineapples they processed at the cannery behind the strange foreigner were sweet and juicy. Since all the folks who worked in the plant got to take some of the fruit home with them at the end of their shifts, he had no doubt Boon Tan had thrown one of those at the stranger.

The man knelt on the ground with a look of sheer bliss on his face as he ate the sweet fruit and sucked on the juice. Jack almost hated to disturb him. He knew a nice fresh Thai pineapple was a true taste treat, especially if you were ravenously hungry, as this poor man appeared to be.

His attempt at stealth didn't last. The guy looked up after taking a good big bite from the fruit, and his eyes landed on Jack walking slowly toward him. Seeing the look of fear on the man's face, Jack attempted to communicate. He held up his hands, smiled, and said, "Don't worry, mate. I'm not going to hurt you."

The guy was silent for a moment, his eyes as wide as half-dollars. Then seeing the smile on Jack's face, his fear seemed to ease a little.

"Hi. I'm Jack."

"Jack?" the man half spoke, half whispered, as if trying the word on for size.

"Yes. I'm Jack," he said, keeping his big reassuring smile in place. "That's me. Who are you?"

The instant transformation that came over the guy's face was unmistakable. He'd gone from surprised to tentatively cautious to terrified, all in a half second. Before Jack could react—damn the hot blacktop and his bare feet—the stranger was on his feet. With both halves of the pineapple still in his hands, he was limping away from Jack as quickly as he could move. Jack couldn't miss that the guy was injured.

Clearly something awful had happened to the poor guy. Jack's instinct was to follow the man and find out what was wrong, offer to help. He didn't have much, but the man running away now had even less, so it just seemed like he needed help. Jack was a fast runner, so he had no doubt he'd have easily overtaken the guy and been able to get him to stop. Unless the guy was too frightened, in which case Jack didn't know what he'd have done. Jack knew scared people, like scared animals, should never be cornered, because they would do anything to get away.

Jack didn't give chase, but simply stood and watched the man limp away. He didn't think the guy would get very far, so he wouldn't pursue him now.

As he returned to his house, Jack quickly ran through the encounter in his mind. What had made the poor guy so scared? He'd spoken Jack's name aloud. English was clearly his native language. But he'd been spooked. What in the world had done it? And then it hit him. The man had gotten scared when Jack had asked him for his name. He guessed he probably shouldn't have done that, because the guy clearly didn't want to reveal his identity. All Jack had been interested in was knowing what he should call the stranger so they could talk. He was quietly kicking himself, even though he couldn't have known it would spook the guy so badly. The man had looked absolutely terrified, which made Jack feel just that much worse.

By the time he'd spoken with Boon Tan—who was still standing outside in her yard, worriedly watching for his return—grabbed his shirt and hat, pulled on his shoes, and returned to where he'd last seen the stranger, the guy was long gone. He wasn't surprised. Jack walked around the area a little to see if he could easily find the guy, but he didn't conduct a rigorous search. When he'd failed to turn up anything after ten minutes, he returned to his house to get in out of the heat.

In this part of the world, if you didn't have to be outside during the hottest part of the day, you didn't spend time outside. Granted, his house wasn't air-conditioned and wasn't a cool oasis, but after living in the country for as many years as he had, Jack's body had acclimated to the conditions. As long as he wasn't in the direct sun, he was actually quite comfortable in his little house most of the time.

Chapter Four
Pineapple

HAD he stayed out in the sun only a little longer, Jack would likely have found him. The man's very sore body hadn't been able to carry him very far as he had fled. He'd been so scared when he first glanced up and spotted someone looking at him. But then he'd recognized the words spoken aloud. After hearing the old lady speak and after seeing street signs, all in some foreign language, he'd been seriously freaked. To finally hear something he recognized had felt so good. It was the first hint of good news he'd had in a couple of days.

But then the man—Jack—had scared the crap out of him by asking his name. How was he supposed to tell Jack he didn't have the slightest idea who he was, where he was, or anything else? He didn't have the answer to that question, so his instinct had been simply to flee.

His hiding spot afforded him a decent view of Jack as he searched. Jack had put a shirt on. The shirt was a button-down shirt, and he had left the buttons undone, affording anyone who looked a good view of his chest and flat abs, not to mention the light coating of blond hair on both places.

He saw Jack wandering around, looking for him, but he stayed hidden. He was terribly torn. Jack was a handsome man, and when he smiled, his face was positively radiant. He didn't seem threatening. If anything, he found Jack the opposite of threatening. He found Jack to be calming, welcoming.

Realizing he'd been admiring a man, he concluded he knew something else about himself—he apparently found men attractive. He didn't know what to do with that fact, but instinctively he knew that was one fact best kept to himself, regardless of the situation.

He continued munching on the best piece of fruit he could ever remember eating. He wasn't sure if it was just because he'd been so hungry or if it really was good. He decided to simply relish the experience and live in the moment. He didn't have much of an alternative. Also, since his memory only went back about twenty-four hours, for all he knew, he ate something this good every day.

When he finished the edible parts of half the pineapple, he tried licking his fingers to get the sticky juice off his hands. He hated having sticky fingers. Since he couldn't very well go back and steal anything else from the old lady's garden, he didn't know where his next meal was coming from or if there would be a next meal, so he decided to keep the other half of the pineapple for a little while. He didn't know how it would keep in the heat, but it seemed to be the prudent course of action.

With a bit of food in his stomach and a quiet, shaded place to hide, he decided to stay put for a time. Leaning back against a brick wall, he fell asleep. He hadn't intended to do so, but something about the heat just made him so lethargic.

He woke several times during the day, but each time he felt utterly listless. He didn't know where he was or where else he could or should be, so he stayed put in his hiding place. It would have been much more comfortable if it had been a soft bed in an air-conditioned room, but that wasn't an option now, so he made do with what he had, which was a piece of dirt under a tree of some sort, beside a wall and behind some bushes. He'd been fortunate to find a break in the fence that allowed him to slip into his hiding place—he'd almost missed it. After he'd slipped through the hole in the fence, he'd been able to bend some of the metal back so it wasn't as obvious to anyone else who might look.

One of the times he woke, he realized it was dusk. He didn't understand how that was possible. He'd slept the previous night, and now he'd apparently slept all day again. He thought about how sore his body was and how much he'd been sleeping, and he wondered if he was ill. He tried to feel his own forehead to see if he had a fever, but it was impossible to tell. He didn't feel feverish, so he didn't know what was going on. He was so confused—and scared. He really wished he had someone he could talk with, ask questions of, get some answers to who he was, where he was, and why he was dressed in such tattered clothes. He looked a wreck. He really hoped this wasn't how he lived all the time. Like stealing the old lady's tomatoes, being dressed in rags just felt wrong.

As the murky gray of dusk turned to full night, he expected the area in which he was hiding to remain quiet. After all, it had been quiet and empty for the entire time he'd been there. But the quiet ended as the first hours of darkness arrived. Cars and trucks came. There was constant noise from cars parking and men and women talking, animatedly in some cases, but all in the strange language he couldn't understand.

He remained hidden in his daytime hiding spot. Feeling hungry again, he picked up the second piece of pineapple he'd kept, brushed off a few ants, and took more careful bites of the fruit. It was still sweet, but it was better when it wasn't so warm.

As he ate, he watched big trucks start to arrive, making lots of noise as they did so. They all seemed to back up and empty their contents into the building nearby. He couldn't see what they unloaded in the dark, but he thought he smelled pineapple. It could be because he'd just finished eating half of one, but he didn't think so. No. The air was permeated with the scent of fresh pineapple.

Whatever the trucks were unloading, a lot of noise was involved. The noise of the truck engines, the beeping of them backing up, the horrendous sound of them lifting and dumping their contents into the mysterious building. And lots of noises from within the building as well.

He was terribly curious. His first instinct was that night meant sleep, but he didn't think he'd be able to sleep with so much noise and so many intriguing things to observe.

He watched and studied everything, from the types of cars and trucks people drove to the characters on the license plates, the way they walked, the way people spoke and interacted. He learned much by observing. He didn't know it, but this was something he'd done all his life.

A war was going on inside his confused brain. Part of him was arguing that the best course of action was to simply stay where he was, out of sight and safe. But another part of his mind argued he should crawl back out of his hiding place and walk around a little bit.

There were so many people out and about that he'd blend in a bit more, he thought, than earlier, when he'd been the only person out, aside from Jack with the beautiful smile. Finally, the side arguing for exploring won out over the side that was afraid and wanted to remain in hiding.

Twisting the pieces of the fence to open the hole once again, he crawled through the fence and stood in the parking lot adjacent to where he'd been hiding. As he stood, he was convinced he smelled pineapple. He wondered if that was what was in the many trucks constantly arriving.

He took advantage of the dark and moved around to various places so he could watch the activity from different angles while remaining hidden. The trucks were most definitely hauling pineapple, lots and lots and lots of pineapple. For hours he lurked in the darkness, simply watching.

A couple of times when a truck came in either too fast or too full, a few of the pineapples spilled out and fell to the pavement below. Each time he raced out of his hiding spot in the darkness and grabbed the fruit. Several times they were smashed beyond usefulness, but he was able to retrieve some mostly intact.

Repeatedly, he raced as quickly as his sore body would carry him back to his hiding space and reached through the hole in the fence to stash his latest find. A couple of times he was convinced someone had spotted him, but they appeared to ignore him, and he went on about his business of retrieving lost fruit.

He lost all track of time and was quite surprised when the sky grew lighter. And then it got brighter. And then the blazing-hot sun was back. He had felt more confident working under the cover of darkness, but now with the light once again chasing away the night, he retreated to his hiding place.

He ate one of his pineapples and then lay down to get some sleep. The heat of the day was overwhelming. Even though he didn't have a pillow or a comfortable bed, he still had no trouble falling asleep.

And that became his pattern for the next three days. During the daytime hours, things were quiet, not to mention hot, and he slept. Each night, people and trucks appeared and there was lots of activity.

At night, he left his hiding place and moved around. He watched. He collected fruit that fell to the ground. Little by little over those three days, he began to feel a little less sore. He still didn't know why he was so sore, and he still had no memory of anything else.

HE thought he was being very careful to keep in the shadows and out of sight for the most part. And he had. But he had been noticed nonetheless. In fact, many people who worked in and around the cannery noticed the guy and remarked about him.

Since he was the only other white guy, everyone wanted to tell Jack what they had seen. Jack didn't know if they assumed he knew who the guy was or why he was out there, but he listened to what everyone had to say and thanked them for their information.

It didn't take Jack much effort to find the man as he scurried around the parking lot collecting fallen pineapples. Standing in the shadows by the loading dock, Jack watched the mystery man carry an armful of the fruits to the ragged old fence surrounding the warehouse and parking lot. He couldn't help but smile as he watched the man loosen a part of the fence and move his daily haul of fruit behind the fence and into the bushes.

Jack didn't know if he would come back out for more. He couldn't imagine how one man could eat so much of one thing, but then he was a good one to talk—he'd lived on the stuff when he'd first started working at the cannery a couple of years ago.

He saw the guy reappear, but only long enough to realize the morning light was imminent. He disappeared back through the fence and reattached it so it looked solid—*sneaky*. When the guy had popped back out, like a gopher popping up out of a hole to take a look around, Jack noticed a couple of things had changed. There was still a hint of a limp there, but it seemed to be much improved. Jack was grateful for that. He hated to see anyone hurting.

Also, the man had lost his jacket and was now walking—no, sneaking—around shirtless. He still had his pants, or what was left of them, on, but the jacket and shirt were now gone. Jack was a bit startled to see that when he wasn't focused on the grease and blood and overall scruffiness, the mystery man was attractive.

The blood appeared to be gone from his face. He'd somehow washed it away. Some of the grease was still there, but one step at a time. Jack gave him immense points for getting the blood removed without running water or towels. He wondered if that was where the shirt had gone. It might have served as a towel to dry his face after the man had washed away the blood from his earlier trauma—whatever that had been.

The night shift was just about concluded. Jack's workday was over, and the cannery was preparing to shut down for the day, which was why he'd been able to stand around looking on the off chance he might see the mystery man. An hour later, Jack was cleaned up from his night of work and had changed clothes. As was the routine of the folks who lived in the little cluster of huts, once a week they made a run to a store to pick up nonperishable food and things they needed. One of his coworkers and neighbors, Sirada, a man about his own age, had an old truck he somehow kept operational. In his free time he tinkered with it and kept it functioning so once each week he could drive everyone to a nearby store to stock up on provisions.

On the drive to the store, Jack was having a ferocious debate with himself about whether or not to take a chance and try to reach out to the stranger. His decision made, he bought a little more than he would usually buy on his weekly shopping trip.

When he got back home, he helped everyone unload their supplies and got his out last. Once he had his own stuff unpacked from the bags and put away the best he could, given his limited accommodations, Jack took a deep breath and said aloud, "Okay, Jackie, it's now or never."

Jack picked up a plastic bag in which he'd placed a few items: several bottles of water, a roll of paper towels, a roll of toilet paper, and some bread. He hoped he didn't scare the guy away, but he felt the most overwhelming need to do something to help the mystery man. He couldn't figure out why he felt so inclined, but the urge just wouldn't leave him.

Maybe it was because his life was incredibly dull and routine beyond belief. He worked, he slept. He worked, he slept. Over and over and over again. He didn't go far or see many people. Maybe he was interested in helping the man because he craved something different in his life, even some little hint of adventure.

For whatever reason, Jack took the bag, grabbed his hat, and quietly walked across the empty parking lot. He stopped at a distance and checked to see if the fence was secure. It was, so he assumed the man was inside. When Jack walked quietly to the break in the fence, he saw how easy it would be to unlatch "the door" and smiled.

It took five seconds to twist the one wire enough for the fence to quietly pop loose. Jack held it tight so it didn't make any more noise than necessary. As quietly as possible, he placed the bag of things on the other side of the fence and then reattached the single wire that held it in place. Given the age and general condition of the fence, it was a miracle it was sturdy enough to stand up to this action. But somehow it did.

Jack turned and walked away. He returned several hours later to see if the bag was still visible—it was not. The bag had been moved and was no longer in evidence. Jack smiled, hoping his gesture hadn't scared the man off but had simply been taken as a friend reaching out a helping hand.

FOR his part, when the man discovered the bag earlier in the day, he'd been startled. No, he'd been more than startled; he'd been terrified. The bag meant someone had discovered him and his hiding place. His first instinct was to immediately flee. But he didn't know where he could go.

His second thought was if someone had brought him a bag of things, they were maybe less likely to cause trouble. He looked inside the bag and saw several big bottles. *Water! Oh, water!* He was so thirsty for water. He immediately opened one of the one-liter bottles and drank for nearly twenty seconds. It was warm but wet, and wonderful.

He recapped the bottle to preserve the precious liquid and checked what else was in the bag. He was delighted beyond words to have toilet paper. Toilet functions had been some of the toughest things for him. He'd hated having no way to clean himself. The paper towels and the toilet paper would make that so much easier. Hell, it would make it possible, which was a magnificent thing.

The last item in the bag was a package of some basic white bread rolls. He held them in his hands as if he'd been given the equivalent of his weight in gold. He simply admired them for a moment before carefully, almost reverentially, opening the package and sniffing.

Yeast. The heavenly smell of yeast. It assaulted his nose in such a pleasant way. Unable to resist the urge, he reached in, grabbed one of the rolls, tore off a piece, and shoved it into his mouth. It wasn't very substantial, so it practically melted in his mouth. Still, it was one of the most wonderful things he could remember experiencing in his very short life.

The first roll was gone in no time. It was quickly joined by a second and then a third. At that point he made himself slow down and then stop. He couldn't just inhale the bread, but it certainly was tempting. It felt so wonderful to be able to pick up a bottle of water, unscrew the cap, and take a drink. He was so delighted with that simple activity he nearly jumped to his feet and did a happy dance.

That afternoon as he slept, he used the roll of paper towels as a pillow. For the first time in almost a week, when he woke up late in the afternoon, his neck was not sore from sleeping in a strange position. Never had he been so happy with something so simple as a roll of paper towels.

It pained him to do so, but he used some of his precious water and sheets of his paper towels to try to clean himself a little. He didn't know where the items had come from, so he didn't know if he'd have any more in future. He had the most overwhelming temptation to hoard what he had, but the thought of being at least a little bit cleaner was just too tempting.

Water. A simple piece of paper towel wet with water and wiped over his body felt so unbelievably good. He wasn't sure, but it was entirely possible he had moaned.

When he was finished, he wondered yet again who had been so kind to leave these things for him. His first guess was Jack, the tall, good-looking man with the strange accent. Not strange so much as simply different from his own. He'd heard himself speak aloud a couple of times, and he'd immediately noticed the difference.

Cleaned up, he sat down to eat while he waited for darkness to fall and bring the start of another day.

Chapter Five
Working the Night Shift

ONCE all hint of sunlight was gone and the activity in the warehouse lot picked up, he crawled out of his hiding place and started his nightly routine. He didn't know why he did it. He had way more pineapples than any one man could eat. In the heat, they weren't lasting that long.

But still, he felt the need to get out and do something, and picking up pineapples and watching people seemed the best thing to do.

He was active at night and still during the day. Only now something new was added to his routine: each morning some new item appeared outside his "door." He could never predict what it was going to be. He found more bottles of water, but in addition to those was always something different. Every morning was a delight with some present to discover and enjoy.

JACK watched and waited. He had been prepared to leave presents every day and not push the man before he seemed ready. So it came as quite a surprise when on the third day, the man spoke first to him.

It was Jack's turn to be startled. He had just opened the fence and was about to leave the gift of the day when he heard the mystery man say two simple words: "Hi, Jack."

His heart pounding, his pulse racing, Jack nearly fell over from where he knelt. When he recovered from his surprise, he looked around and quickly spotted the man. He'd used the razor Jack gave him the day before to shave, so his face was smooth. Jack was nearly speechless.

"Wow!"

"Wow?" the man parroted back to him. "Wow what?"

"Wow, you're a very good-looking man."

"I am?" he asked Jack.

"You are. Very."

Most people would take that as a compliment, but those words only made him sigh deeply.

"What did I say wrong?" Jack asked.

"Nothing," he answered Jack sadly.

Jack didn't know how far to push. There were so many unknowns involved. He decided he had to try. "I don't believe you," Jack said as gently as possible.

He looked up at Jack, stared intently at him. It gave Jack his first really good look at his eyes. They were intense, a beautiful blue like the sky on a gorgeous, bright fall afternoon.

Jack gasped.

"What's wrong?" the man asked, concerned.

"You have absolutely beautiful eyes, mate."

"I do?"

"You do."

"I didn't know that."

"I don't want to scare you off. I hated how you ran last time. It was the last thing I wanted to do."

"Why are you being so nice to me?" he asked Jack.

"You just seemed to need it."

They were both quiet for a minute. The man had his head down, but at least he hadn't taken off running again. A moment later he surprised Jack when he said, "I do."

"We all need help in some form."

He considered Jack's statement, surprised by the depth of those simple words. He remained quiet but contemplative.

Jack didn't trust the silence, so he spoke again. "Can we begin again?"

The man nodded.

"Hi. I'm Jack. What's your name?"

Even though he'd prepared himself for the question, it still made him wince and draw back a little bit.

"I did it again! I'm so sorry," Jack said, a look of sheer horror on his face. "Please don't run away. I'll shut up and leave you alone if that's what you want. I'm sorry. Whatever I said, please—"

"I don't know," he whispered.

"Excuse me?" Jack said, his voice only slightly louder.

"I ran because of your question. Because I don't know the answer."

Jack looked confused.

Wanting Jack to understand, he continued, "I don't know my name. I don't know anything about who I am. I don't know where I am. I don't know anything about myself. I don't know where I've been. I don't know where home is. I don't know why I'm here. I don't know anything about who I am. And until you, I haven't been able to understand a single word anyone has said to me. I'm so scared, Jack."

Jack was speechless. He hadn't seen this coming. "I'm sorry," he offered. "That must be… awful."

He nodded. "Yes, it is."

When those eyes looked up at him next, Jack saw the fear in them. He couldn't begin to imagine how terrifying it must be to be lost—lost not just from everyone and everything you know, but from yourself as well. He didn't think about it before acting. Jack stepped forward and wrapped the man in a hug. He couldn't find words appropriate to the moment, so he just kept his mouth shut and spoke with his body instead, gently hugging the stranger.

Jack heard him crying. "I'm so scared, Jack. I'm so scared. What do I do?"

"I know you are. I wish I had the answer, but I don't. What I do have are two arms to wrap around you and hold you so you're not so alone. Can I be your friend?"

He stopped crying and looked at Jack, pausing only long enough to wipe away some of his tears. "Why?"

"Why what?" Jack asked.

"Why would you want to be my friend?"

"I'm a good judge of people. I think you're a good person. And you and I are alike in that we're basic white guys in a land where there aren't that many."

"You must have lots and lots of friends," he protested.

"No. Some, yes, but not lots. We all need friends. I need friends as much as you do. Will you be my friend?"

"Okay." He nodded without hesitation.

"Good. Now that's settled, will you join me for breakfast?"

Smiling at Jack, the man nodded in agreement. "Yes. Yes, I'd like that. Very much."

Jack returned his smile. They rose to their feet. Jack put his arm around his new friend's shoulder and held him close while also leading him across the now empty parking lot.

"So what am I going to call you? I haven't had a buddy in so long, I don't know…," Jack asked.

"That's it. Buddy. Would that work?"

Jack chuckled at the idea. "I suppose it would. Buddy. All right. That works for me."

"Me too," Buddy said.

Chapter Six
Rescue, of a Sort

EVEN though he'd been hanging around the area for a week now, Buddy hadn't seen much about where the people nearby lived. He'd seen the little houses they lived in, but not the insides of those houses. The one time he'd wandered too close, a pineapple in the back had taught him—don't go near the houses.

When Jack led him into his home that morning, his guest was rather surprised. From the outside the place didn't look like much of anything, but inside it was actually rather nice.

The space was not huge. Everything needed for living was in one single, exceptionally well-organized— and much to his surprise, very pleasant—room. For some reason, he'd expected the places to have dirt floors, so he was startled to see a wooden floor. He was even more startled the little house had electricity. At least he assumed there was electricity because the ceiling fan was running, creating a cool, gentle breeze.

Against one wall, Jack had a small table with two chairs, which was apparently where he took his meals. He instinctively looked for the kitchen but failed to find one.

Jack was apparently observant or at least able to make a good guess. "Thai homes don't have the same kitchens as Western homes."

Buddy paused, deep in thought for a moment. "How did I know to be surprised? How did I know what to look for in a kitchen? How did I know what was missing or different?"

"I don't know," Jack answered honestly.

Feeling uncomfortable, Buddy decided to make a joke, or try to anyway. "How are you going to make breakfast for us if you don't have a kitchen?"

It was obvious to Jack what Buddy was trying to do. Jack let the subject drop for the moment, moving instead into tour-guide mode. He showed Buddy where the small dormitory-sized refrigerator resided. He pointed out where the sink could be found, as well as the food storage for nonperishable things.

"You obviously see the bed," he said, gesturing toward the double bed against another wall. In addition to the table and the bed, the room was fairly simple, with two comfortable-looking chairs separated by a small table with a lamp and a bookcase.

"Oh," Jack said, suddenly realizing he'd forgotten one important point. He grabbed a part of one wall and shoved it aside to reveal the bathroom. It was ultra small, but it had everything a bathroom should have: a sink, a toilet, and a shower stall.

Smiling at him, Jack said, "Now, if I was a betting man, I'd put money on the fact that a shower would feel mighty good to you about now. Would I be a winner?"

Nodding, Buddy had a look of sheer awe on his face. "Oh, yes." He didn't even think about it before he slipped off what little clothing he had on and immediately entered the shower. He made absolutely zero effort to close the door or to make any move toward seeking privacy, not that Jack was objecting. Buddy turned on the water and just stood in place, allowing it to gently wash over his dirty, disgusting, and grimy body.

Even with the gift of bottled water and paper towels, he still felt grungy beyond belief. The combination of not having had a shower for—well, for who knew how long—with the heat and humidity of the local climate would make anyone feel less than optimal.

Jack stood transfixed by the vision of the man showering in front of him. He was completely oblivious to Jack's or anyone else's presence. He had given himself over utterly to the feel of the water cascading over his body, caressing him like a long-lost lover.

Buddy's eyes were closed and his head thrown back, the water gently falling first on his head and then slowly down his body. Every drop took away more grime and dirt, washing away some of the accumulated bad things that had happened to him over the last week—or however long it had been. Maybe, just maybe, if he scrubbed away enough, he might even find out who he was. Between the wonderful feel of the shower and the thought of learning his identity, Buddy had to smile.

If Jack had been transfixed before, now the guy was wet, hunky, and happy, Jack was a goner. He sighed. This mystery man was absolutely gorgeous. Jack knew he needed to get his lust under control. He knew the surest way to freak out a man—any man, potentially—was to come on to him unexpectedly. And Jack didn't want to risk chasing this poor lost soul away again. So he summoned every ounce of strength he had and tried to take his mind off the gorgeous man in front of him. The guy had shed his few remaining clothes so effortlessly and with absolutely no hesitation. And what a body he had beneath those clothes!

He was tall, well-built, with a light coating of hair on his torso and around his crotch. His legs appeared to also have a light coating of blondish hair, but Jack couldn't be entirely sure. He also didn't want to risk looking any closer. Jack stepped away from the small room to let his guest enjoy his shower in peace, but it suddenly occurred to him that they hadn't had rain in a couple of days. Since his and all the other houses in the cluster relied on rain for their water, he quickly dashed outside, climbed the ladder to the roof, and checked the level of his water supply.

"Oh bloody hell," he muttered—one, because he had to tell his guest to turn off the shower, and two, because he had to look at his wet, naked guest again. One would disappoint Buddy, and the other would challenge Jack. But he had no choice. Better to warn him now than have him find out the hard way. Jack quickly descended the ladder and made his way directly to the small bathroom.

"Sorry to interrupt," he said, trying to avert his eyes.

"I'm sorry," Buddy said automatically. "I should have checked with you before just hopping in here. I'm so sorry. That was so thoughtless of me."

"No, no. Not a problem," Jack tried to assure him. "I know I'd want a shower if I was in your position. The problem is we're just about out of water." He reached into the shower stall, trying desperately not to touch the gorgeous naked man in his shower, and turned off the water. "I recommend you soap up, with the water turned off. Scrub everything that needs scrubbing, and then rinse off all at once and quickly. Think you can do that?" he asked with a smile.

"Of course. I'm so sorry for using all of your water."

"Not a problem. Trust me, we'll have more than enough soon. We are in Thailand, after all."

Buddy looked up, evidently startled. "Thailand. Is that where we are?" Even with his eyes wide, the mystery man was gorgeous.

"Yes. We're just outside of Bangkok, Thailand."

"Thailand," he said, as if trying the word on for size to see if it fit. "Thailand," he repeated. Jack got the impression the word meant nothing to him. He slowly shook his head, and his look of peace and tranquility from the shower was replaced by one of sadness.

Jack tried to nip it in the bud before it got worse. "Don't worry about that right now. We'll deal with it later. First, you should scrub." He picked up the bar of wet soap and handed it to Buddy, who took the bar and returned a smile. Jack had to quickly retreat from the room. In the main room of his house, he stood with his back against the wall, his head thrown back and his eyes closed. He tried focusing on his breathing to get himself under control.

"Come on, Jack," he spoke aloud. "Get it together. So you've got a gorgeous naked man in your shower and you haven't had sex in a long time. Keep it together, and don't scare the pretty man away again. He's got enough shit to deal with right now." His pep talk completed, he took a deep breath and stood away from the wall. He heard the shower come back on for maybe fifteen seconds and then turn off again. He had to smile; the guy was trying so hard.

"Um, Jack?" he heard his guest say from the bathroom.

"Yes?" Jack asked, popping back into the doorway.

"Do you have a towel I could use, by any chance?"

"Oh, yes, so sorry," Jack said, grabbing a towel from a nearby shelf. He didn't have much, but he did have a second towel. He was counting on the guy using the towel to cover himself so Jack could have some chance of surviving without jumping the poor guy's bones. He handed the towel to the gorgeous naked man in his shower and then nearly moaned in frustration as he put the towel over his head and slowly dried his hair and face. Jack had no alternative but to look down at Buddy's body, and what a body he had. Whoever he was, he had spent some serious time keeping himself in shape. Many men their age were dealing with the early onset of middle-age spread. But not so for this man. This man was well put together and had kept himself in good shape—no, great shape—somehow. However he had done it, it worked. Jack guessed his guest was close to his own thirty-two years. He wished he looked as good, though.

Jack had tried so hard not to look, but he was only human. His eyes settled naturally onto his guest's crotch. While not huge, what nested there was thick. Jack unconsciously licked his lips, wishing he could drop to his knees and take the man's penis into his mouth. The way it sat atop his balls, arching out and down slightly, was so inviting. Jack felt his knees wobble a bit, but fortunately he remained upright.

He raised his eyes back to Buddy's face just a second before the guy brought the towel down to wipe off his legs, slowly and carefully, which forced Jack once more to study his body. *Damn!* he thought. He turned and left Buddy to his tasks, only to have to turn around and go back into the bathroom.

"So sorry to bother you again, but you probably would love to brush your teeth as well." He reached under the sink and extracted a brand-new toothbrush, still sealed in its original packaging. Jack made the mistake of looking up at his guest while he was kneeling to get under the bathroom sink. The move placed his face directly in line with the man's ample and attractive penis. Jack had to get out quick. He placed the toothbrush on the sink counter and pointed to the toothpaste. "Got you all set up here. Let me know if you need anything else."

"Jack. Thank you so much. I don't know why you're being so nice, but I am forever in your debt."

Jack thought the guy could repay some of that debt by lowering the towel from shoulder level so it covered his tender bits—his beautiful, attractive, desirable tender bits—but he didn't say that. Instead he smiled and turned to leave the room once again. He tried to busy himself in an effort to keep his mind, and his libido, off the naked man just a few feet away.

One of his neighbors owned a good-sized flock of chickens, which kept their little community in fresh eggs. He walked over to her house and got a few from the most recently laid eggs to prepare for his guest and himself. Back at his house, he turned on the gas grill outside and quickly scrambled the eggs. At the same time, he toasted some bread to make the classic eggs and toast breakfast.

He turned off the gas and carried things back into the house. "Plates would be nice," he said to himself. He dished things up and placed the plates and accompaniments on the table.

"Breakfast is served," Jack said to his guest, indicating he should take a seat. Jack was desperately trying to ignore the fact that Buddy was naked except for the towel wrapped around his waist—the towel *precariously* wrapped around his waist.

They were both quiet for a moment while they tasted the breakfast Jack had prepared remarkably quickly.

"Oh," Buddy moaned with a look of ecstasy on his face.

"What's wrong?" Jack asked, concerned he'd done something terribly wrong.

"Nothing. Nothing is wrong. Not one thing. This tastes so good. After living on pineapple for so long, this is phenomenal. Thank you, thank you, thank you." To show his appreciation, the man practically inhaled the eggs and toast. Jack admired the speed with which he ate.

"I guess you were hungry," Jack said, stating the obvious.

"I am such a happy man," Buddy said with a shy smile that Jack found absolutely adorable. "A shower, great breakfast, a shower, a new friend, a shower…."

"I see a theme here." Jack snickered with him. "Once we get some rain, I promise you can take a shower again."

When both plates had been cleared, they sat quietly for a moment, savoring a cup of tea Jack had brewed while he had the gas grill running. He'd learned to be very efficient with his cooking.

Chapter Seven
A Good Day's Sleep

FOR Jack, one of the best parts of any meal was the tea that followed. That morning as he sat quietly savoring his cup of English breakfast tea, he almost missed the fact that his guest had become increasingly quiet. When he realized Buddy was just about to fall asleep, Jack mentally chastised himself for not anticipating something so obvious. That didn't change the fact, though, that he was unsure how to handle the situation.

He most certainly was not about to send Buddy back out to sleep on the ground under a tree, especially when the rain that had avoided them all week long was predicted to start. Somehow—and here was Jack's problem—somehow the two of them were going to have to sleep together. Jack prayed he wouldn't make a fool of himself and scare the poor guy away yet again.

Buddy was already skittish, so Jack kept up a quiet mantra in his head to not hump the pretty naked man in his sleep. He hoped maybe there was a chance he would do the right thing.

Touching the guy's bare shoulder to rouse him from his slumber, Jack said, "Hey. Sorry to wake you."

Before he could continue, though, Buddy stood and said, "I should be going."

"Um," Jack started as Buddy headed for the door. "You might want to rethink that."

"Huh?" the obviously sleepy man said.

"Two problems. One, you're dressed only in a towel, and two, we're supposed to get rain sometime today. We need it to replenish our water supply, but still, you can't sleep in the rain where you've been sleeping. So I want you to crawl into bed and get some sleep." He gestured toward the bed.

Buddy was clearly going through a torrent of emotions. They could all be compressed to a fairly simple dichotomy: the bed looked incredibly welcoming after sleeping on the ground for who knew how long, and the bed was not his.

"I can't take your bed," he said, that side of the internal argument winning.

"You are not taking it. I'm inviting you to share it."

Before he could stop himself, Buddy burst into a huge smile and quickly closed the distance between them so he could give his one friend in the world a big hug. He was so happy that he lifted Jack up off the ground and spun him around—not an easy task, since Jack was not a small man. Still, though, Buddy was bigger.

Jack was convinced he was on the expressway to hell when his guest set him back down and Jack noticed the towel had come loose during his excitement, and Buddy seemed absolutely fine about that.

"I don't know what to say," he said to Jack. He crossed to the bed and ran one hand over the sheets. He touched the pillows with reverence. Watching him, Jack knew that regardless of the cost to him personally, the guy had to sleep there with him. No one should have to sleep on the ground, especially someone such as the vision of loveliness in front of him who had had so much stolen from him.

"Which side do you sleep on?" Buddy asked, pulling Jack from his ongoing internal monologue.

"Um, I usually sleep alone, so I tend to move around a bit, but I always start out on the right side."

"Okay. May I?" he asked as he moved to stand on the left side of the bed.

"Yes, please," Jack told him, admiring the view from the backside of his guest as much as he had the front. Buddy carefully lifted the sheet and did some combination of sliding and crawling into bed. Whatever you called it, it worked for him—he moaned audibly as he lay back. He placed his head on the pillow on his side of the bed very carefully.

"I'm in heaven," he said. He glanced across the small room, and Jack nearly melted from the look he got. He didn't know Buddy—and apparently he didn't even know himself—but the only way he could describe the look he was getting was sultry. Buddy lay on the bed, his feet tucked under the sheet but the rest of him uncovered. The room was quite warm because it was the middle of the day and hot outside.

Jack didn't think Buddy meant to be so seductive, but as Buddy tossed back the sheet on his side of the bed and patted it, smiling up at Jack—causing serious melting—Jack didn't know how much longer he could be accountable for his actions.

Jack decided he had to just get it over with, so he latched the screen door, turned his back so his guest wouldn't see the obvious swelling in his crotch, dropped his clothes, and crawled quickly into bed. Step one accomplished. They were both lying on their backs. The only difference was Jack covered his lower body with the sheet. He needed the shield in case he popped an erection. In case? Who was he kidding? When, not in case.

Jack closed his eyes and tried to think nonsexual thoughts, but that plan only worked for about fifteen seconds. He jumped with surprise when he felt a hand on his hands, which were folded across his flat belly.

"Seriously, Jack, thank you. I can't begin to tell you how much better this feels than where I've been sleeping."

"No problem, my friend."

"Why are you being so nice to me?" Buddy asked again, still obviously not believing his good fortune.

"You looked like you needed a friend."

Jack thought that might be the end of the conversation, and for twenty seconds it was. But then Buddy spoke again. "You don't know me. Hell, I don't know me. There are so many things I don't know, but I do know you have been nicer to me than…." He was silent for a few more seconds. "Thank you. Anything you ever need—or want—is yours. I mean it. If I have it or can do it, I'll do it for you."

Jack felt himself shudder. *Oh, sweet Jesus!* he thought. *This man is offering me anything. He might even be willing... no!* He scolded himself for even considering the possibility. And his scolding was working until the guy spoke again.

"Seriously. I owe you, Jack." He rolled to his side, toward Jack, looked at him, his hand still on top of Jack's hands, and continued, although his words now were barely a whisper. "I've been so scared, Jack. So scared. I've felt so alone. I didn't know—I don't know—who I am, where I am, what I'm doing here. You've helped me more than I can tell you."

Jack turned his head toward his guest, rolled over a little toward him, smiled, and said, "I am delighted to be of assistance." He decided a little honesty wouldn't be a bad thing. "You see, you're not the only one who's been alone."

"You too, Jack?"

"You don't see another person living here, do you?" he asked.

He looked around. "No." He was quiet for a few minutes before asking, "Jack?"

"Yes?"

"I know you need to sleep, but can I ask you a couple of questions?"

"Sure. I'll answer if I'm able."

"You said we are in a place called Thailand?" Buddy asked.

"That's right. Just outside of Bangkok, Thailand."

"I wonder why I'm here. I haven't understood a single word I've heard people speaking until I met you. When you spoke to me and I understood the words you said, I was so excited and so scared all at the same time. I don't belong here—in Thailand. It wasn't until I met you and spent time with you that I finally got comfortable. I like talking with you. I like being with you. I'm very comfortable here in this bed with you...."

Oh, sweet Jesus, Jack moaned to himself. When he spoke aloud, he said, "You could have been here on holiday or business when something happened to you. Your clothes looked like you'd been through the mill. They were all torn and scuffed and were a mess. I'd guess you were in an accident of some sort. Maybe you were in a building that burned down. Maybe you were in a car accident. I don't know. I'm just tossing out some possibilities."

"I understand," he said seriously, with an almost reverential tone as he spoke to Jack.

"Let's get some sleep. I have to go to work at eleven tonight."

"I'm keeping you awake, Jack. I'm so sorry."

"Not a problem, mate," Jack told him with a reassuring smile. "As much as I'm able to, I'll help you figure things out. But for now, just feel safe and comfortable and get some rest."

"Thank you," he whispered. Those were his last words before he fell asleep.

Jack was exhausted after a hard night of work, but he had a harder time falling asleep. The room felt hot, he felt hot, the bed felt hot. But that was illogical. The room was the exact same temperature it had been the previous day. Jack had lived in Thailand long enough to be fully adapted to the heat and humidity of the country, so it wasn't external temperature that was getting to him. It was the beautiful man sleeping just inches away from him. Jack had not been lying when he'd told Buddy he'd been alone. He should have said it more bluntly: he'd been lonely too. If the man hadn't been a complete stranger, he might have told him a little bit more about his circumstances. He wasn't ruling out that possibility, but not until he knew the guy a bit better, assuming there was enough of him left to get to know. *That was too harsh*, Jack scolded himself. Buddy was missing his memories, but his personality was still there, and his personality seemed to be one of a sweet, sweet man. Jack fell asleep that morning telling himself he would do whatever he could to help the handsome stranger in his bed.

Chapter Eight
A Shower

WHEN Jack woke up that evening, he was at first very surprised. No, *surprised* was too mild a term. Shocked would be more appropriate. In fact, he might even have jumped a little as he tried to figure out what was going on.

Jack had lived alone for quite a long time, and in that time he hadn't entertained any gentleman callers, so he was quite shocked to wake up and find another person curled around him.

As he got over his initial shock and figured out what was going on, Jack relaxed a tiny bit—but not completely. Just because he knew who was wrapped so tightly around his body didn't solve everything. He still needed to decide how best to handle the situation.

Jack lay still, running a huge number of possibilities through his mind, trying to figure out the best course of action. He had to admit it felt nice—really, really nice. It had been so long since he'd felt the tactile sensation of a man's body, and he missed the feel of someone so fully in contact with his own. Every sensory nerve in Jack's body was basking in the closeness of his mysterious houseguest.

He tried to be as still as possible, even though the more primitive parts of his brain were telling his body to grab ahold of the man behind him and try to pull him even tighter—assuming that was even possible. He had tried not to move, but apparently his guest was waking on his own. It was about time to get up anyway. Jack had sort of thought Buddy might sleep in a bit, because he must have been tired from sleeping on the ground for so long.

Jack heard him make a sound that was neither a moan nor a purr, but more somewhere between the two. Since Jack didn't know much of anything about the handsome stranger in his bed, he didn't know if Buddy was going to freak out when he woke up to find another man in his arms. When he remained calm, Jack was mightily relieved. Thinking back to the clues he'd had earlier in the day, he really shouldn't have been surprised. Buddy had, after all, felt zero reluctance about walking around naked or nearly naked. And Jack certainly wasn't going to complain that the sexy man wanted to hold on to him.

"Morning," Buddy said close to Jack's ear.

"Morning," he answered. "Sleep well?"

"Fantastic!"

"Good." Jack was very pleased with Buddy's reactions. The guy hadn't jumped or jerked away, didn't seem repulsed to be touching another man. Jack was proud of himself for keeping it together so well, but he very nearly lost it when Buddy tried to pull him closer rather than push him away.

They lay together in bed, both apparently relishing the feel of the other. The predicted rainfall had started sometime while they'd slept.

"It's really coming down out there," Buddy said.

"Typical Thai rain. It may be gone fairly quickly, but I hope it goes on long enough to fill up the water tanks again."

"Oh, right," he said, recalling the abbreviated shower that morning. "Is the rain cold here?" he asked, raising his head but still holding on to Jack.

"No. There's nothing cold in Thailand at this time of the year."

Buddy relinquished his hold on Jack and rose to kneel on the bed beside him. Jack turned to look at him and saw an expression of incredible excitement on his face. He looked almost impish, not to mention slightly aroused.

"What's going on in that mind of yours?" Jack asked curiously.

"Can I shower outside?"

"What?"

"Can I go outside to shower? I would love to wash some more. Can I take the bar of soap and go outside? Will that scare anybody?"

"In most parts of the country, you probably shouldn't do something like that, but the group that lives here is pretty laid-back. If you just go outside the front door, it shouldn't be a problem."

As if to affirm his idea, the rain picked up in intensity. Buddy bounded off the bed, grabbed the bar of soap from the shower, and dashed out the front door.

Jack was so curious he had to get up and go look. The sight that greeted him was of a full-grown man acting like an adolescent. The guy looked so happy.

Jack leaned against the doorframe and watched Buddy put his head back, raise both his arms out to his sides, and delight in the feel of something so simple as water.

As he watched, Buddy looked toward him, smiled one of his million-dollar smiles, and held his hand out to Jack.

"Jack, this feels fantastic! Come on out and join me."

Jack normally wouldn't dream of doing anything of the sort, but that evening, as the rain fell and the light gave way to dusk and then night, he decided a little unconventionality was called for occasionally. He didn't have anything to take off, so he simply stepped outside and let Buddy take his hand to pull him out to where he thought Jack would get the most water.

He couldn't help himself—Jack laughed. Maybe even giggled. It felt so… youthful, irresponsible, and frolicsome—he loved it! As if Jack weren't getting wet enough just from the rain pouring down from the sky, Buddy caught some water in his cupped hands and delighted in throwing the water at Jack. He of course had to repay the favor in kind. The two laughed uncontrollably. Jack hoped his neighbors wouldn't be too freaked out by the sight of two naked men in the rain.

Buddy twirled himself around a full three hundred sixty degrees, with his arms completely extended. Jack chuckled. He instinctively reached for the soap and started to try to wash away a bit of dirt on Buddy's side. Whatever it was, it didn't come off very easily, so he had to scrub quite a bit. Buddy held still so Jack could wash his back.

HAD Jack been able to observe Buddy's face, he would have seen a look of sheer delight. The feel of Jack's hands on his back just felt so good, so natural. Buddy didn't know all the details, but it felt like he'd found something that had been missing from his life. He didn't know whether he had someone who did this for him at home, wherever home might be, or if he just simply liked the feel. He had so much to figure out and didn't know where to start. But he did know that now was not the time. Now was the time to wallow in the glory of nature's shower, and it certainly was glorious.

When Jack was satisfied he'd gotten the dirt, or whatever it was, off Buddy's back, he reached down and patted Buddy's butt and said, "Okay. All done."

Rather than be offended, Buddy turned around and took the bar of soap from Jack's hand and told him to turn around. Jack was surprised and caught off guard. It all happened so fast he simply complied with the request.

As he stood there in the rain that evening and felt the large hands of the beautiful stranger rub over his neck, his shoulders, his back, Jack felt himself melting into the touch.

Buddy picked up on how positively Jack responded to his massaging Jack's shoulders, so when he finished washing Jack's back, he returned his hands to Jack's shoulders to slowly work the muscles. It felt like he was tense, so Buddy did his absolute best to try to help Jack relax at least a little bit. When he felt he had done as much as he could, Buddy wrapped his arms around Jack's body briefly, hugged him, and then went back to scrubbing with the soap.

As quickly as he soaped up, the rain rinsed it away. By the time they were finished, the rain seemed to be winding down.

"That felt wonderful," Buddy said as they headed back into the house.

Jack went inside and grabbed two towels from the bathroom. He took one, quickly wiped away the rainwater, and then handed the other to his guest, moving out of his way so he could come fully inside as well.

When they were dry, Jack returned the two towels to the bathroom. When he came back into the main room, he grabbed a pair of skimpy shorts he sometimes wore and pulled them on. He thought he had a second pair, and while it took a little bit of looking, he found them. He held them up to Buddy's torso and guessed they would fit him. They would be a little tighter than he might like them in the ideal world, but they would cover him up, assuming that was of interest to him.

"The clothes you had on when you arrived were a bit of a mess. I hope you don't mind, but we can try to clean them if you want to wear them again."

"I don't want them. They don't mean anything to me." Buddy sighed. "I went through them over and over and over again, hoping I would find something that might identify who I am."

"No luck?" Jack asked.

"None. No wallet. No business card. No name written on anything. No identification of any sort. I couldn't even tell you where they were made. I thought that might help. But nothing. Absolutely nothing."

Jack was concerned Buddy was going to spiral into a really depressed mood, so he tried to shift the subject and get his mind off his identity, or more properly his lack of an identity.

"Hungry?" Jack asked.

"Yes, I am, actually. What do you typically eat at this time of day?"

"Well, I think you've probably guessed by now that I'm not a wealthy man, so I don't do extravagant things. One of my favorites is a pineapple fried rice with little bits of meat stirred in—sometimes chicken, sometimes shrimp, sometimes pork."

"Sounds incredible. I'm guessing that getting fresh pineapple is not too difficult around here."

Jack laughed. "No. Quite the opposite, which is why you were able to pick up so many over the last few days."

Buddy raised himself up to his full height in surprise. "You mean, people saw me?"

"Yes. Everyone saw you. Everyone kept coming to me to ask who you were."

"Why you?"

"Look at us. We are the only two white guys you're likely to see around here. People saw you and assumed you were with me."

"People saw me?" he asked again, surprised his stealthy behavior hadn't worked better.

"Yes," Jack answered with a hesitant smile. Buddy seemed surprised, so he had to be careful not to embarrass him.

"Don't worry."

"I'm sorry."

"For what?" Jack asked, honestly confused.

"For causing you so much trouble."

"You haven't caused me any trouble whatsoever."

He seemed not to believe Jack, so Jack decided to put him to work on helping with dinner to take his mind off things.

"I could use some help cutting up the pineapple," Jack announced, more as an order than an invitation.

"I don't know if I've ever cooked anything before in my life," Buddy apologized. "I might not be much help."

"Well, there's only one way to find out," Jack told him, guiding him to a cutting board, a knife, and an intact pineapple. He explained how to go about the task and demonstrated before he turned Buddy loose to do it. Jack watched carefully to make sure he didn't do something to show he had no business being in the kitchen. But Jack was pleased; his guest seemed comfortable with the work and didn't exhibit any problem whatsoever.

While Buddy peeled and diced pineapple, Jack prepared the rice and the meat to use that day. Twenty minutes later, they sat down to a plate full of rice in front of each of them.

"Wow!" Buddy pronounced. "Looks fantastic! Smells even better."

They both took bites and pronounced it as good as it looked and smelled. Jack insisted Buddy drink as much water as possible. "Trust me," he informed Buddy. "I've lived here long enough to know what the tropical heat can do to a man."

When dinner was finished, he showed Buddy where he stored his massive amount of bottled water.

"You look like you're prepared for a while," Buddy observed approvingly.

"I pick up more whenever I get a ride to the store. It's too heavy to carry when I walk."

"Where do you shop? How do you shop?" he asked curiously.

"One of the folks here has a truck. He drives all of us once a week, and we stock up as much as possible. The truck is old, but the man who owns it does an amazing job of keeping it running. Someday it will break down, and then I don't know what we'll do, but we'll worry about that when the day arrives. No sense worrying about it until we have to."

Buddy seemed contemplative. "Wise words, Jack," he said softly.

They cleaned up the dishes from dinner and put things away. Buddy could see that order and organization were important when living in so small a space. There just wasn't room for a lot of clutter, and a day of dirty dishes piled up would qualify as clutter.

That task finished, Jack had some time before he had to report to the cannery that night. They sat on the bed facing each other. "I work starting at eleven each night, six nights a week. I get off at seven in the morning. You know the pattern, since you've followed it for the last week. We work when the day is at its coolest and sleep when the heat is the worst."

"I'll go back to my little spot while you're at work, Jack."

"Why?" Jack asked, honestly confused by the statement.

"You'll be out. You don't want a stranger in your house while you're not here."

"I shared my bed with you last night. That seems far more intimate than leaving you in my house while I'm at work. And besides, you've seen the place. I don't have anything worth stealing." He thought a joke was in order. "And if you did rob me, I'd be able to find you. You're a foot or two taller than most Thai, and you'd kind of stand out anywhere you tried to go around here."

His joke sort of fell flat, although he wasn't sure why. "You should stay here while I'm working. I've got some books you can read. No TV. Sorry."

"You're sure, Jack?" Buddy asked.

"Of course. If I wasn't sure, I wouldn't have made the offer."

"Is there anything I can do for you while you're working tonight?"

"Um...." Jack hesitated, not entirely sure what to tell him. He wished he had something to have him do, but he didn't know what it would be. If it were a normal house, he might have a washing machine and could have Buddy do laundry. A normal house might have more space that needed cleaning. But he didn't have a normal house. "Nothing I can think of offhand. While I'm working, I'll think about it and see if I get any brilliant ideas."

"Okay." Buddy got up and looked at Jack's books. He could read the words, but he didn't have a clue if they were familiar to him or not. "I think I'll read if that's okay. Maybe I'll find something that triggers a memory."

"That's a great idea," Jack concurred. "While I'm working, I'll also see what I can think of as a way to start investigating who you might be."

Buddy's head jerked around so quickly Jack was concerned for a moment that he might suffer whiplash. "You... you might help me? To find out who I am?"

"I make no guarantees we'll succeed, but we can try."

THAT night while Jack worked, Buddy read. During the middle of the night, he took a break from reading to go back to the spot where he'd slept earlier in the week. The pineapples were rotting quickly, and he felt he should do his part and put them into a dumpster. It took him a while, but he got them all cleaned up. He was a bit surprised by how many he had accumulated in such a short time. Those that looked in good shape, he carried back to Jack's place and piled them against the wall in front of the house.

He also hauled back the things Jack had bought and given to him, and brought out the empty containers of the things he had used up, like the bottles of water Jack had given him. As he carried them to the dumpster, he reflected on how very lucky he was to find someone as nice as Jack. He could just as easily have found someone who would take advantage of him, and how would he know? He knew he needed a friend if he was going to survive for more than a few days. And he was especially going to need a friend if he had any hope of finding out who he was.

Chapter Nine
You Came Back!

THE cannery operated from 11:00 p.m. to 7:00 a.m. A few minutes after seven, when Jack returned from work, Buddy greeted him at the door much like a dog greets his human with a reaction like, "Oh! You came back! I'm so glad to see you!"

Jack almost laughed but was able to contain his reaction when they greeted each other. Who knew how Buddy's ego would handle laughter when he was the subject?

After they washed up the breakfast dishes, they both showered—separately, of course—and then crawled into bed. Jack hadn't slept super well the previous night, partly because of sheer lust and partly because he was terribly out of practice at sharing his bed with another person. He hoped to sleep better that night.

Before going to sleep, though, Jack shared one bit of news with Buddy. "I talked with some of my coworkers today about whether or not any of them knew of any accidents that might have involved any Westerners. When you first appeared, you looked tattered and battered and somewhat the worse for wear. That plus you were limping."

"Right. For several days I was really sore and achy. I had a lot of cuts and bruises too. I have no idea why."

"This is just guesswork, but it seemed possible to me that you were in some kind of accident. Based on how you looked, if it was an accident, it wasn't a simple little fender-bender, but was something serious.

"It turns out there was a big accident somewhat near here around the time when you appeared. A taxi—which fits—was involved in a huge wreck."

"Really? Could that help us somehow?"

"I hope so. I've got some people checking to see if they can find out some more about the accident—where, what time of day, who was involved, was anyone injured, things like that. If the name of the taxi company and cabdriver are known, then we can maybe track backwards and see where he was driving that day."

"Thank you, Jack. You… you've just been so good to me. I don't know how I can ever thank you enough."

"Don't worry. Let's just go to sleep." Jack was secretly thinking, *You can repay me by rolling over here and locking those hot lips of yours on mine*, but he managed to keep those thoughts tightly bottled up inside his head. Little did he know the man lying in bed next to him had the same thoughts, only from his perspective, he desperately needed Jack's help and absolutely did not want to do anything to piss him off. And while Buddy might not remember who he was, one thing he guessed was that leaning over to kiss a naked man who did not want to be kissed was not a good way to win friends and influence people, unless the influence you were aiming for was to bug the crap out of them.

Chapter Ten
Worry About Tomorrow When It Gets Here

LATER in the afternoon, when their day of sleep was finished, Buddy woke first. It was raining once again. A gentle rain this time, rather than the torrential downpour they had experienced the previous day.

After a quick trip to the bathroom, he made his way quietly across the room to stand in the open doorway. Leaning against the doorjamb, he watched the rain but also was completely unaware of it. He was so scared. He felt so desperately helpless. He was so alone, even though another man slept just a few feet away. Nearly in tears and shaking with fear, he hugged his arms around his body and just listened to the rain hitting the ground.

He felt such an overwhelming attraction for Jack. Buddy might not know his own identity, but his dick definitely knew what he liked. But he didn't dare dream of acting on those urges. If he did anything wrong, he'd be back living under a tree in the bushes beside a parking lot and eating what he could pick up off the ground.

He didn't even realize he was doing it, but tears were running down his cheeks. He hugged himself a little more tightly and tried hard to tamp down his fear. He was so focused on his inner turmoil he missed the sounds of Jack waking up, getting out of bed, and walking across the room.

It wasn't until Jack stood right behind him and touched his shoulder that he realized he wasn't alone. He didn't mean to, but he jumped in surprise at the feel of the hand on his shoulder.

When he turned around, Jack saw the tears Buddy thought he'd felt.

"What's wrong?" Jack gently asked. "Are you okay?"

"No," he answered, the tears still rolling down his face.

"What's wrong?" Jack asked again, wrapping his arms around the trembling man in front of him. "Whatever's wrong, we'll fix it. Please tell me."

"Jack," he whispered, "I'm so afraid. I'm so scared. Except for you, I'm all alone… and I'm so lost." He stood still and simply enjoyed the feeling of Jack's arms around his body.

"Shh," Jack said, trying to calm his fears. "You're not alone. I'm right here. We'll get through this together."

But for some reason, Jack's words were not comforting him. "Jack, what if I do something to upset you, without even realizing I've done it? I wouldn't mean to make you angry, but you could throw me out and I'd be all alone again."

"Hey, hey, don't even think such things. You haven't done anything to upset me—just the opposite. You've been a great addition to my life. I wasn't really living before you got here—I was just existing, just going through the motions for lack of anything better to do. Your arrival has been good for me."

Jack continued to hold the man as he cried. Slowly, ever so slowly, Buddy stopped shaking and his tears gradually lessened.

"I want to tell you something my grandmother used to tell me," Jack said as he released him and stepped back a few inches so he could look at his friend's face.

"What's that?"

"She always said, 'Don't worry about tomorrow until it gets here. Today has quite enough concerns of its own. Deal with today before worrying about tomorrow.'"

"She sounds like a very wise woman."

"She was." Jack held his hands on Buddy's arms, prepared to bring him in for another hug if necessary.

"Thank you, Jack," he said softly. "Thank you so much for everything."

"Not a problem. I'm delighted I can help in some small way."

"It's anything but small."

Jack was desperately in need of stepping away. Holding the naked man had been tough enough, but to have to stand there, naked, and hear him speak about things being "anything but small" just about sent Jack over the edge.

He quickly excused himself and stepped into the bathroom, where he tried desperately to get his hyperactive libido under control. It was too bad there was no such thing as cold water in Thailand—what he needed was to be able to take a very cold shower to shock himself into behaving. The poor man in the other room had enough crap to deal with at the moment. He certainly didn't need the only person he knew coming on to him and scaring him even more.

Jack had barely managed to get away before his erection gave him away. When he had the thing under control, at least momentarily, he opened the bathroom door and quickly exited to grab a pair of shorts. His guest was still naked. It was most unfortunate that the man looked so absolutely gorgeous and stunning as he stood by the door waiting for Jack to return.

To help take his mind off the issue, Jack busied himself preparing their evening meal. Cooking for two meant he was going through his supplies faster than usual. Jack was thinking that when he finished work the next morning, it would be necessary to make a run to the local market. He slipped away for a moment to ask his neighbor with the truck if he'd be willing to drive Jack to the market a couple of days early. If it had been just himself, he would simply have made do or walked, but since he was responsible for this other man, he wouldn't even think about asking Buddy to go without for a couple of days, and he didn't want to leave him alone any more than he already was.

That night, while Jack worked, Buddy sat and read more books. Reading was the only thing he had to do, and he was so grateful he hadn't lost the ability to read along with his memories.

In the morning, when Jack returned, he informed his guest of the need to make a run to the market and invited him to go along. Since Buddy had not been anywhere, he gladly agreed to accompany Jack.

Even if Buddy hadn't wanted to, he would have felt obligated to go along to help Jack haul things home. *Home.* He hadn't intended to, but Jack's place was the closest he had to "home" at the moment. Home was here because he and Jack were here.

For Buddy, the trek to the market had been exhilarating and scary all at the same time. The area outside the cannery was somewhat deserted and quiet, except for the ever-present highway noise. But there were no pedestrians and not even sidewalks in the predominantly industrial area. But the area around the market was quite different, crowded, noisy, and busy. The truck in which they rode was indeed ancient and barely seemed up to the task, but it got them where they needed to go and back again. Jack and Buddy sat in the back end of the truck, while others sat up front with the driver.

The market was equally scary because it was so busy and everyone was speaking a language Buddy couldn't understand. Even the most basic things were confusing to him. None of the cans made any sense. None of the smells seemed right. Nothing was familiar. Absolutely everything was frightening to him, even with Jack just a few feet away. The trip to the market was meant in some ways to be a treat for him, but it only served to reinforce his need to bottle up his physical feelings for Jack.

FOR the next few days, Buddy was hypercautious about everything. He tried to remain quiet and out of the way as much as possible so he wasn't a problem. He thought he was being discreet, but in reality his behavior was anything but discreet.

Finally, Jack couldn't take it any longer, and when they crawled into bed, Jack asked, "Before we go to sleep, can I ask you a question?"

"Of course, Jack. Anything. I'd do absolutely anything for you."

Jack mentally kicked himself for walking right into that one. After taking a deep breath, he plowed forward. "Are you okay? Have I done something to upset you? Is something wrong?"

"No! Jack, no!"

"You've been so very quiet the last few days. I've been worried."

He looked down, unable to meet Jack's eyes. "I'm sorry, Jack."

"No. Don't.... Just tell me. Please, you can talk to me absolutely anytime about anything. You don't need to hold things back." Jack tried to smile reassuringly. When Buddy wouldn't even look at him, Jack gently reached for his chin and lifted his face until they were able to look at each other. "What's caused this change of behavior?"

"I'm just trying to stay out of the way as much as possible. You had your life, and I've just dropped myself right into the middle of it. I'm just trying to be as little trouble as possible," he explained. "I feel bad that everything is on you, all the cost of food and other things. I wish there was some way I could help out."

"Okay. First, you are not trouble in the slightest. You have been a great addition to my life and my little home. Second, you are a wonderful man, and I'm delighted to have you here to talk with and just be with. Don't worry. Please relax, talk to me about anything at any time, and be direct with me. Okay?"

He shyly nodded, smiling at Jack. "Okay, Jack. Thanks."

"Okay. Tell you what, when we need some help at the cannery, I'll come get you some night and you can help out and earn a little money. Would that be all right?"

"Yes! Absolutely. Thank you, Jack."

"Don't thank me until you've worked a shift. It's a lot of heavy work."

Jack turned away so they could both go to sleep. He was surprised to feel Buddy roll behind him and grapple him in a hug as they lay in bed. Jack nearly shivered with frustration. When he felt Buddy's lips gently kiss his neck, his dick simply said *To hell with this* and sprang forth into a rock-hard state.

Jack was so very relieved when Buddy released him and rolled over to his own side of the bed. When he was sure the man had fallen asleep, Jack quietly crawled out of bed and made his way to the bathroom, where he desperately jerked off to try to ease his horniness.

He had gone a couple of years with no sexual partners. He kept lecturing himself that he absolutely had to get it under control.

Little did he know that just a few feet away, Buddy was awake and having much the same conversation in his mind. He'd slipped that morning when he kissed Jack's neck. He mentally scolded himself for screwing up in such a near-catastrophic fashion.

Neither of them slept well that day.

Chapter Eleven
Scene of the Accident

ONE morning when Jack returned from work, he seemed more pensive than usual. When questioned, he couldn't hide he was troubled.

"Jack? What's wrong? You seem upset."

"I am. And no, it's nothing you've done. Relax. I'm upset because I learned something today."

"What?" Buddy asked, his fears only partially allayed.

"I talked with some people and learned a little more about the auto accident I was telling you about, the one that happened a few weeks back. There's a bunch of different stories making the rounds, but my best guess after listening to all of them is it started when a car, maybe a taxi, ran straight into a truck. Whoever was driving the car died immediately. That car caught fire and was barely recognizable as a car after that, so no one is sure of anything. Given where it happened, coming in from the airport, it sounds possible it could have been the car you were in and you'd just flown into the country from somewhere else."

Buddy sat silently, taking in all this new information, trying to slot it into the few memories he had, memories that appeared to begin just after… whatever had happened.

"I had some burns," Buddy said out of the blue.

"Excuse me?" Jack asked.

"I remember I had some burns—on one leg. And the pants, if you can call them that, had a burn hole on one leg. Whatever happened to me probably involved a fire."

"And remember how torn up your clothes were," Jack said.

"I remember," Buddy quietly concurred.

"It looked like you'd had to crawl out of a well, or out of a… a…. I don't know what."

"Maybe out of a burning cab," Buddy said softly.

"Do you remember that?" Jack asked hesitantly, knowing how frustrating the lack of memories was for Buddy.

"No. I don't remember anything. That's the problem. I'm just guessing. You know, trying to put the pieces together into some logical order. You've got to agree I wasn't dressed like anyone else. It looked like I'd had to pull myself out of something with a lot of sharp, hot edges that tore up my clothes and burned me somehow."

Jack nodded solemnly. For some time this had been Jack's working hypothesis. He'd just never brought it up for discussion because he knew how

much it upset his new best friend to not know what
had happened to him.

"Do you know where the accident occurred?"
Buddy asked.

"Yes," Jack said softly.

"Is it far?"

"About a mile or so." Jack knew where this was
going, and he was not anxious to help it along in any way.

"Can you take me there?"

"Yes. But I'm not sure…. Are you sure you want to
go there, to see it?"

"Yes… maybe it will remind me of something."

"First, we're not even sure you were in that car,
we're not sure it was a taxi. We're not sure you were
even in an accident." He knew as soon as he spoke the
words aloud that it was a useless argument. "Okay. I'll
take you there."

"When can we go?"

"Now?" Jack said. Usually they would eat breakfast
and then go to bed, so this was a dramatic departure from
their routine. Since Buddy spent most of his time inside
Jack's house, he usually didn't wear anything during
the bulk of his day. The climate was so hot he simply
remained naked in an effort to stay comfortable. Jack
gave him a pair of loose cotton pants and an old button-
up shirt to go with a pair of sneakers, a bottle of water for
each of them to take with them, and they set out to walk
to the scene of the accident.

The constant traffic was noisy. The air was rank
with smog and car exhaust fumes. The sun and the
constant humidity made the walk grueling. It wasn't a
long distance, but it was far enough, both physically as
well as psychologically.

When Jack stopped walking, Buddy looked around, not understanding why they were stopping at first.

"Is this where it happened? How do you know this is it? I can't see anything that makes this look any different than that piece of road over there," he said, gesturing off to his left.

"Yes. If you look carefully you can still see some of the skid marks on the road surface," he said, indicating the marks that were obvious to Buddy once Jack pointed them out. The two of them stood side by side, looking at the markings on the busy roadway. "I think it started over there," Jack said, turning to what was left of the original skid marks. "My best guess is the car you were in got pushed that way, got hit by at least one other vehicle coming from the other way. What happened next… who knows for sure? But somehow the cab wound up way down there," Jack said, pointing to a spot some distance away, a spot still clearly scarred by scorch marks from a very hot fire. There was no question where the accident had started and where it had ended.

It was only because rush hour traffic was gridlocked and at an absolute standstill that they could walk around and look at everything. Had traffic been moving, there was no way they could have walked where they did that morning. Still, they moved relatively quickly because the road surface and all the vehicles were radiating heat into an already overheated atmosphere.

After maybe five minutes of walking slowly and looking in silence, Jack asked, "Triggering any memories at all?"

Buddy simply shook his head. Clearly this expedition had been a failure. He'd been so hopeful as they had headed out to visit the accident scene. Partly he felt good just to be doing something. He'd felt so helpless before. Without realizing it, he had placed a great deal of emphasis on this outing, so when the visit to the site failed to turn up anything, he felt doubly depressed.

Jack didn't push, letting him take all the time he needed to look. It was only when Buddy was ready that they left to return home.

They were quiet on the walk back to the house. Their return trip was the same distance as the trip there had been, but it took nearly twice as long because they walked more slowly since it was hotter. For one, the day had heated up substantially in the time they'd been at the scene of the accident. To not overheat too badly, they walked at a slower pace. They were also both somewhat distracted during the walk back.

Buddy was quiet the rest of that day. Jack tried to be a comforting presence for the man who had unexpectedly become his best friend, but it was difficult to console him in the place he was at that particular point in time. Jack was feeling quite inadequate at helping his friend, so when they went to bed that morning he did the only thing he could think to do.

Jack approached him tentatively. First he lay behind Buddy, gently placing a hand on his arm just to offer the assurance of a touch. When he didn't object or pull away, Jack slowly increased their body contact, moving from having just his hand on the man to wrapping his arm around him, then to hugging him while their two bodies touched in as many ways as possible. What happened next started so quietly that at first Jack wasn't even aware of it—Buddy was crying.

Instead of providing comfort, Jack seemed to be having the exact opposite effect.

"I'm sorry. I didn't mean to make it worse."

"No, Jack, I'm the one who's sorry. You've been so good to me, and all I can offer is a broken man who isn't even able to…."

"Shh," Jack whispered. He held on and let Buddy cry. He wished he had the perfect words of wisdom to fix the man's problems, but he didn't. All he could offer was a stronger hug.

Jack kissed Buddy's neck, the only part of his friend's body he could reach with his lips, but didn't think Buddy noticed; he kept crying, though a little softer than before at least.

He continued gently stroking Buddy where he was able to reach—his arm, his chest, his belly. It seemed to be helping.

And then it happened. About ten minutes after he'd wrapped himself around his friend, Jack was softly caressing Buddy's stomach—he had always admired those abs. Moving his hand a little lower, he unexpectedly brushed against something. *Oh crap!* Buddy had an erection, and Jack had just touched it.

With a mind of its own, Jack's dick rose too. The only problem was he was wrapped around his friend, and Buddy's arms were holding tightly on to Jack's. He wanted to get away, to run, to hide, to get someplace where Buddy wouldn't see what was happening to him. But he knew that to pull away from Buddy in his current emotional condition could do more damage, so he stayed in place.

They lay perfectly still for a moment. Without realizing it, they both had also been holding their breath. Then each finally exhaled. Jack didn't know what to do. Buddy didn't either, but he made the first move. He didn't know what words would work in the present situation, so he simply put his hand on Jack's arm and gently stroked his fingers along it.

Jack shuddered at the lightest of touches. Taking the touch as the okay he hadn't expected, Jack kissed Buddy's neck once again. At the same time, his hand that had accidentally bumped Buddy's erection moved back there, this time deliberately. Even though Jack was excited beyond belief, he gently wrapped his hand around the thick, hard rod. It was a question as to which of the two of them sighed first.

Not caring, Jack rolled Buddy over onto his back and pulled himself on top of Buddy's prone body. His lips sought the other man's, unable to focus on anything other than trying to meld the two of their bodies together into one in every way possible.

After weeks of looking and longing, they were both seriously aroused for each other and could finally express what they were feeling. They kissed, they rolled around, first one on top and then the other. The sheet that had covered them was kicked to the side. Their hands explored each other's body, caressing, stroking, pulling.

Their long-awaited first sexual experience was relatively short-lived. Both men were so aroused that once they started to kiss and roll around against each other, it took very little time for both of them to experience an orgasm. After it was over, neither knew who had ejaculated first, and it didn't matter.

It took a few minutes for them to get their breathing under control and for their hearts to slow down.

"I've wanted to do that since the first time I saw you," Buddy said to Jack.

"Really? Me too."

"Really?"

"Oh, yes. You've had me so fucking hot for so long now."

"I wish I'd known."

"Likewise," Jack said with a smile that threatened to split his face in half.

"The key thing is that you know now."

Ignoring the stickiness between their bodies, they pressed together in order to kiss once again. This time their kiss was more tender—at least at first. Slowly, their tongues probed each other, carefully constructing a dance for two.

It didn't take long for their kiss to reawaken the two sleeping giants between their legs. Buddy maneuvered them so he was on his back and Jack was on top of him. Without breaking their kiss, he lifted his legs and gave Jack a clear indication of where he wanted him to be relatively soon.

Jack broke the kiss momentarily. "I don't have any lube." He nearly cried in frustration.

Not to be deterred, Buddy rolled out from under Jack, jumped up, and dashed into the kitchen. Jack looked to see what he was doing but wasn't able to tell. A moment later Buddy returned, proudly holding up a perfectly reasonable lube substitute—a bottle of peanut oil.

Buddy had also thought to bring a towel to the bed with him, so when he pulled Jack back between his legs and liberally coated the man's rock-hard erection with oil, the bed was spared from getting oily as well.

They kissed once again. Jack felt Buddy doing something. His brain was so fogged with lust it took him a moment to figure out Buddy was loosening himself up with the oil.

Buddy was smooth. His task completed, he moved his hand to pull Jack up against his body. Jack resisted at first. This was too sudden. He needed to talk with Buddy first. They needed to have some ground rules. Unfortunately, though, his dick was working on a different set of guidelines; it had one prime directive— to slam inside the man's body and do what it was designed to do. Period.

And that was precisely what happened. Buddy guided the head of Jack's erection to him, then grabbed Jack's butt with both hands and pulled his lover inside his body. While their kiss continued, they both gasped as they felt the other's body.

Buddy broke their kiss reluctantly when he arched and threw his head back. Jack froze, convinced he'd hurt the man, but when Buddy moved so Jack could see his face, there wasn't a trace of pain or anxiety or anything negative. The only thing he could see was sheer ecstasy.

Jack's mind might have been hesitant, but his body knew what to do. They began to move together as one. Jack tried to be slow at first, but that just wasn't in the cards that day. If he didn't go fast enough or slam himself hard enough into his friend's body, Buddy practically begged for him to do it.

"Oh God, Jack! Fuck me! Please! Fuck me! Fuck me! Fuck me!"

"Anything you say."

"Fuck me like you're meant to fuck me."

"Anything you want, baby."

Their lips came together, so Buddy's hands had to take over while his mouth was otherwise engaged. Somehow the man folded himself more tightly over so Jack was completely on top of his body. More than he ever had, Buddy felt safe, covered and protected by Jack while he shared himself. Jack was his everything, and he wanted to do whatever he could to show him how much he appreciated what he'd done over recent weeks.

Buddy loved the safe feeling he had with Jack in charge. Jack knew what he was doing, and for once Buddy also knew what he was doing. And it felt fan-fucking-tastic. He didn't want this to ever end.

Pulling his lips from Jack's, he grabbed Jack's head and stared into his eyes. The look of lust he found there was matched only by his own. "Give me everything you've got. Do it. Ride me like there's no tomorrow. Ride me like this is the last night of our lives. Breed me like you know you've wanted to all these weeks. Do it. Do it now."

Whoever would have guessed that quiet Buddy was such a noisy, demanding lover? The dirty talk only succeeded in spurring Jack on to fuck him harder. Jack was quietly grateful none of their neighbors spoke English. There was no mistaking what they were doing, but at least the neighbors wouldn't have every detail. Such was the price of living so close together.

With Buddy still holding on to Jack's head and staring into his eyes to tell his friend he meant every word he said, Jack put his hands on Buddy's shoulders and started pouring on even more energy and enthusiasm. Their two bodies slammed together with enough force to register on the local seismic monitors. Jack pounded into his friend's ass with such gusto the headboard of the bed slammed rhythmically and repeatedly into the wall behind where it usually sat quietly.

"Yes! Jack, that's it. Take me. Make me yours. Yes, yes, yes. Fuck me. Shove your dick up where it belongs," Buddy demanded. "I can take everything you've got. Give it to me. Give it to me hard. I've wanted this for so long. I need this. Now. Hard. Please."

Jack was absolutely not going to stop. His genitals were 100 percent in charge, and they were stimulated like they hadn't been in years. There was no way this mating was going to stop until a whole lot of testosterone was removed from his system.

When it happened, it hit Jack fast. When he felt the telltale signs of an approaching orgasm, Jack tried to slow down for a moment, maybe prolong the bliss he was feeling. But there was no way that was happening. He was too far gone. A few seconds later his eyes rolled back in his head and he piston-pumped his dick as deep as possible into the body of the man beneath him as he erupted. Over and over and over again his body shuddered, jerked, spasmed as he fired an untold amount of semen deep into his lover's body.

Jack held himself still for a moment, and then simply fell forward onto Buddy, gasping for breath. Panting, Jack didn't move. He couldn't. And why would he want to?

Neither of them said a word for several minutes, both simply basking in the sensations that continued to wash over their bodies. In a barely audible voice, Buddy whispered into Jack's ear, "I can feel your heart beating against my chest."

Jack turned his head so he could see the man's face. He smiled. His smile was returned by an equally happy smile.

"Thank you, Jack. I've wanted you so badly."

"I'm yours, babe. I'm yours."

"Ditto."

Jack's erection was shrinking. Buddy wasn't ready to let go just yet. He very smoothly flipped them over so Jack was lying on his back with Buddy sitting on top of his crotch. Using the muscles in his ass, Buddy very carefully massaged the shrinking dick.

Jack wasn't entirely sure how it was possible, but his lover's gentle manipulations were getting him hard again. Buddy took his time and slowly and gently worked on Jack's penis, walking it through long and swollen to turgid and all the way to rock-hard and ready to rumble.

Once he felt Jack back to full mast, Buddy started to lift himself up off Jack's erection and then slowly sink back down. The oil he'd started with earlier combined with the jism Jack had already given him to lubricate their next mating.

Up. Back down. Up. Down. They had both come once. Jack had come twice, so there was no urgency this time to fuck like rabid animals. Slowly, Buddy fucked himself on Jack's erection, watching the face of the man beneath him. Jack's eyes were closed, but he was very much awake and aware of everything happening.

Languidly, Buddy grabbed his erection as it bobbed around each time he sank back onto Jack's dick. His hand, still with oil on it, slowly stroked his dick in rhythm to the rest of their movements. Buddy's eyes were closed, and his body seemed to be working on autopilot.

For nearly twenty minutes Buddy rode Jack's rod until once again Jack went from vague rumblings of an orgasm straight to an ejaculation that felt like his entire body was turning itself inside out and shooting into the other man's body.

Jack reached up, grasped Buddy's shoulder tightly, and held the man still while he gulped in air, his body spasmed, and then he fell back to lie flat. Neither man spoke. Jack focused just on getting some air into his lungs and getting his heart rate to slow down. His eyes were closed, so he failed to see Buddy start to lean toward him. His eyes fluttered open in surprise when he felt the man's lips on his.

Gently, ever so gently and delicately, Buddy kissed him. There was no rush, there was no race, there was no hurry. Their kiss was a statement of simple pleasure and comfort. Buddy leaned forward as much as possible and rested his head on Jack's shoulder.

They fell asleep in that position. Sometime later they separated without either really being aware of the movement. When they woke, Jack was lying on his back and Buddy was sleeping against his side with his head on Jack's chest. Jack reached a hand out and touched Buddy's hair, as if to see if the whole thing had just been a really vivid dream. But no. The hair was real. The man was real. Buddy was real. It had happened. Jack was very happy. Jack was falling in love.

Chapter Twelve
Waking to a New Life
and a New Love

"WHAT do I do now?" Buddy asked Jack a few days after their trip to the accident site.

"We should probably start by going to the embassy for your country."

"And what is that? Am I American? Am I Canadian? Maybe I'm British. Aren't those the choices you named off for me when I first got here?"

"Sounds about right. You could also be South African or something else. I don't know. My best guess, and mind you, it's only a guess, is that you're an American. So we could start by going to the US Embassy," Jack suggested.

Buddy was silent for several minutes before he asked, "Where are you from, Jack?"

"Australia."

"And if you were in my position, would you go to the Australian Embassy for help?"

"No. I couldn't. My embassy... well, let's just say I left Australia for a reason, and because of that I've overstayed my visa. If I went to them, they'd be obliged to get me out of Thailand and back to Australia. I might be able to go back now, but I'd rather not test that just yet."

"No!" Buddy shouted, panic evident.

"It's all right, mate. I'm not going anywhere."

"Don't leave me, Jack! Please. I'm begging you. Please don't leave me here alone. You're... you're the only person I know."

"You know our neighbors," Jack suggested.

"Sure, I recognize them, but we can't communicate. Only you and I can talk." Buddy was quiet, clearly deep in thought. "What if I did something, you know, something wrong, something bad, or maybe I overstayed my visa? Maybe they'd try to take me away from you, Jack. What would I do? I don't know anybody but you. I don't know any place except this place. This is all I know, Jack. I don't want to go to any embassy. What good would going there do anyway?"

"What if I went to visit the American Embassy to ask some questions, see if anyone is looking for you? Would that be all right?" Jack asked.

"Don't tell them where I am, Jack. Please. I don't want anybody to take me away from you. Promise?"

"I promise, mate. Don't worry."

THAT week, Jack and Buddy were out every single day for at least a couple of hours doing something to investigate Buddy's origins.

One day they checked newspaper reports from the time when Buddy had first appeared to read about the accident and to see if there were any reports of missing people. Jack guessed Buddy was American, based on his accent. So they focused on reports of an American who'd been involved in anything, Americans who had gone missing at around the time they found each other. That turned up absolutely nothing, not even a hint.

Another day they took a bus a different direction and visited television stations, continuing their quest for any reports of a missing American. Each time they hoped for answers but came away disappointed.

Day after day they trudged along, taking buses that covered the city. Jack had assembled a seemingly endless list of things and places they should check. One day they even went to the airport and walked all around the international arrivals area, hoping something might trigger a memory in Buddy's head.

While they were there, Jack walked up to any customer service person they could find with one simple question: "Do you recognize this man?" It was a long shot, given the thousands of people who passed through the airport every day, but it was something Buddy was comfortable doing.

They didn't limit their questioning to people behind counters. They talked with janitors, people who handled baggage, people who worked the taxicab lines outside. They talked with everyone they could find with the same simple question.

Jack cautioned Buddy to not expect anything from time spent at the airport, but Buddy was comfortable with it. The airport was huge and had an unbelievable number of airlines, so it took them several days of many hours to work their way through all the possibilities. Since flights were coming and going all day and night long, they varied their search hours so they covered all parts of the workday to be sure to catch everyone who worked there.

On their next day of "airport duty," as they had come to call it, they finally found a clue. The only problem was they didn't know what to do with that clue.

After only an hour of walking and talking—well, Jack talked since he spoke Thai and Buddy did not—they finally found someone at one of the first-class check-in lines who said, "Yes, I remember him. He's flown through here before. I'm positive of it."

Even though Buddy couldn't speak Thai, he could tell just from facial expressions and body language they had found something. It turned out the woman they were talking with from United Airlines spoke flawless English, so they switched over to English so Buddy could participate in the conversation.

Excitedly, Buddy asked, "You recognize me? You know me? You know my name?"

"No, sir. Unfortunately I do not know your name. But I do remember seeing you. And there have also been people here over the last month showing pictures of you and asking questions."

Buddy didn't know what to say; Jack did. "Hey, mate! Someone's looking for you! This is great news." Buddy still didn't know what to make of the news.

"Who has been looking for me?" he asked.

"A private investigator as well as the local police, both some time ago and then again just recently."

"Well, it sounds like you're an American, my friend," Jack said, trying to sound upbeat.

"Sounds like a strong possibility."

"Do you have a name of who is searching for me?"

"They left a card. Give me a moment to look in the back."

The woman was gone for several minutes. When she finally returned, she was empty-handed.

"I'm so sorry, sir, but the card is not where I left it. Someone must have moved it. If I can find it, how should I reach you?"

Buddy looked worriedly at Jack.

"We don't have a telephone," Jack explained. Thinking quickly, he left the main phone number for the cannery where he worked and asked that they call that number. He cautioned her that the place kept unusual hours, so it could be difficult to reach a person directly.

Finally with some good news, they called it a day and headed home. Jack noticed Buddy was very quiet on the way home. He finally asked, "What's wrong?"

"What if people are looking for me because I did something awful? What if I killed someone? Or robbed a bank? What if people are searching for me to arrest me? I remember running to get away from something." Jack saw tears in his friend's eyes, so he put his arm around Buddy's shoulders. "What if someone is after me to kill me?"

"I suppose that is a possibility," Jack offered. "I hadn't thought about it," he added, considering the idea for the first time. He didn't really think that was the case, but it did give him pause while the idea worked its way around inside his head.

BACK inside the comfort and safety of their home, Buddy lay in bed and felt Jack crawl in, equally naked, to lie close behind him. Jack's strong arms went around Buddy's body and held him tight. It was clear their mini success had triggered an entirely unexpected set of concerns and issues.

Jack hadn't thought about the fact that Buddy might possibly be on the run from bad guys. If that was the case, then they could very well have just painted a great big neon sign pointing them straight to where their target waited for them. Jack didn't voice those concerns. He didn't want to add to the anxiety his lover was already obviously feeling. They simply lay in bed for a few minutes without either saying a word.

Buddy got out of bed for a moment but quickly returned. Once again, back pressed tightly to Jack's front, they rolled over so he lay beneath Jack's body. Jack felt a telltale slickness. How had he done that? Jack needed to watch him more closely. Somehow he'd lubed himself. He wanted Jack inside his body. Jack was only too happy to comply.

While they'd been out crisscrossing the city in search of any clues as to Buddy's identity, they had stopped in one of the many little stores they passed and bought a container of lube. When Jack picked up one, Buddy smiled, put it back, and grabbed the next bigger size, the largest the store had available.

No words were needed since their bodies knew the steps to this dance. Without hands, Jack's erection found where it needed to be to press entry into Buddy's beautiful body. Jack had lost track of how many times they'd lain like this over the last week. However many times it was, Jack never got tired of the feeling. Each time he slipped gently into Buddy's body it felt like a thousand tongues licking his body or a thousand tiny hands masturbating his erection.

Buddy clearly loved getting fucked, which was fine with Jack, although he quietly hoped sometime they could switch so he could feel the other man's arousal slide into his own body. Buddy had a beautiful erection. Hell, the man had a beautiful everything. Sometime when they caught up to where their libidos needed to be, he'd bring up the idea, but not now. At the moment he was balls-deep in his lover's ass and he had no need to think. All he wanted to do—all he needed to do—was to experience the feel of their two bodies joined in the most intimate fashion two humans could become one.

Neither of them moved for the longest time. Jack's erection throbbed a few times to tell him it was still awake and ready for action, but otherwise they simply lay connected. Jack could quite comfortably have fallen asleep like he was at that moment. He was happy.

And apparently he did fall asleep—both of them fell asleep. When he woke later, they had slipped apart, but they still lay cuddled together, with Jack behind Buddy.

For years Jack hadn't lived but had simply existed. He'd been hiding out from life and from the pains of life for too long. While the original cause for him fleeing home was long past, he had no desire to return to Australia. His life was in Thailand now. With Buddy's unexpected arrival, his life had reawakened from its self-imposed stasis, and he suddenly remembered how life could sometimes be good.

Without even realizing he was doing it, Jack's first response upon waking with his arms around the other man was to smile. A simple smile, but all that needed to be known. Jack was happy once again.

Chapter Thirteen
Searching for the Lost Sheep

DAY after day, Jack got up and went to work at the cannery. Buddy stayed home wishing there was something he could do to help out financially and otherwise. Several times, as he had mentioned earlier, Jack came home after starting work and asked Buddy if he wanted to help out in the cannery. Anytime someone didn't show up for work or called in sick, Buddy helped out, in the process earning some money.

When they weren't working, they followed their new routine. Instead of coming home and going to sleep, Jack came home, showered, changed clothes, and they started out. Some days they halfheartedly searched for any clues to Buddy's identity, but mostly they played tourist, checking out some of the local sights.

When they finished their traipsing around the city, they returned to the house to sleep through the hottest part of the day. Buddy was becoming more discouraged. He so desperately wanted to know who he was, but with each passing day, he felt the trail to his real identity grow colder and colder. It almost felt like his identity was being pulled further and further away from him, to the point he would never be able to find out who he was.

Weeks after they had started their quest for Buddy's identity, Jack one morning told his lover he needed to go check out one lead on his own. Buddy was confused, concerned, worried, and about a dozen other emotions that were all layered atop one another. Even though his face said otherwise, Buddy didn't object or question Jack's decision. He knew wherever Jack was going, he had a good reason, and Buddy simply had to trust the man. So he did.

Jack's mission that day was simple: he went to visit the United States Embassy in Bangkok. Jack had never been to the United States. He was not a United States citizen. He had no clue how easy or difficult it might be to get inside to talk with someone. The answer was that it was both. He had no problem talking with someone, but talking with someone who could actually answer his questions? Well, that was an entirely separate matter.

After an untold number of hours spent standing in lines, Jack was shuffled from one place to another, each with its own line. When he'd asked someone if the lines were unusual, the answer he got was no; budget cuts had reduced staff, which meant everyone who came through the doors had to be more patient.

Jack shared the account of the situation several times but got nowhere with anyone. Jack had finally had all he could take for one day. He left in the heat of the afternoon, knowing no more than he had earlier in the day when he'd first arrived at the embassy. As he made his way home that afternoon, he did know one thing he hadn't known earlier: apparently it was not unusual for Americans to simply disappear in Thailand.

Over and over again that day he'd heard embassy personnel say a number of people, usually men, traveled to Thailand and then simply went under the radar for some time for a host of reasons. He'd heard how they almost always reappeared when they ran out of money and their local prostitute kicked them out, having sucked them dry—of funds.

Jack was very cautious in his approach to the entire issue. He never clarified he was not trying to locate someone who was missing but was trying to find a listing of those who had been reported missing. He didn't explain, but he was hoping to be able to match his friend by photo or description. Unfortunately the embassy would not provide him with that information, citing privacy laws and concerns.

On the off chance the man who had been living with him for more than a month was in some serious trouble with the law or someone worse than the law—as Jack had been in Australia—Jack was very careful to not provide too much information. Had he known that several of the people he spoke with that day had photos and descriptions of his friend sitting mere inches from where he'd sat to ask his questions, he would have been a most unhappy man.

WHEN he got to his little house that afternoon, Buddy was sitting outside in the shade of the house waiting for him. The moment he saw Jack, he was on his feet and was racing toward the man, grappling him in a hug that lifted him off the ground.

"Hey! Hey!" Jack said, gently. "What's wrong?"

"I was so worried you weren't coming back, Jack. I was so scared."

"Of course I came back. I wouldn't leave you." He stepped back a half step and smiled at Buddy. "You can't get rid of me that easily." He'd meant it as a joke, an attempt to lighten the mood, which was extraordinarily heavy and concerning. His attempt at levity apparently failed, because he found himself grappled in another near bone-crushing hug.

"Shh. Shh. It's okay," Jack said repeatedly into his friend's ear until he finally calmed down a little bit.

When Buddy released his hold on Jack—actually, he maintained his hold, but he at least put the man back down on the ground—they went into the house and out of the hot afternoon sun.

Since he'd been out and about, Jack was hot and sweaty. As he shed his clothes, he headed directly into the bathroom; he desperately needed a shower. He didn't like to waste the water, but that afternoon he felt he had earned the luxury of a second shower. He washed quickly to preserve their water supply.

As he had anticipated, when he turned off the shower and stepped out, Buddy was standing immediately in front of him, waiting. He held out a towel, which Jack gratefully accepted.

"Thank you," Jack told him, slipping forward to give him a quick kiss on the lips. He knew if anything would make the man smile, a kiss would. He was not disappointed when the smile appeared. Shyly Buddy dropped his head as if embarrassed. Jack lifted his chin upward and gave him another kiss, this one a little bit longer than just a peck on the lips.

Together they retreated to the main room of the house and sat at the table. Buddy had food waiting for them. He'd needed to keep busy that day, so they had a great deal of very good food prepared.

"Where did you go today, Jack? And did you find what you wanted?"

Jack had expected the question.

"I went to your country's embassy to ask some questions and see if I could get a list of people who had been reported missing. Maybe see some pictures, read some descriptions."

His friend's face was immediately lit up with excitement. "And?"

"I know you've been concerned maybe someone is looking for you because you're running from the police or did something that makes you a wanted man. So I thought it would be easier for me to walk in and ask some questions than to have you walk in and say, 'Hi, folks. Am I a wanted man? Do you have my picture on your most-wanted list?' See what I mean?"

Buddy nodded. "I understand now, Jack. I wish you had told me, though. I was a nervous wreck all day long, not knowing where you were or what was going on."

"I see that now. And I'm sorry I didn't tell you. I should have. I'm sorry for being so thoughtless, leaving you back here not knowing. I promise not to do that again."

He gave Jack another small smile. "Thanks, Jack."

They were quiet for a moment before he repeated one of his earlier questions. "Did you find what you wanted?"

Jack shook his head slowly. "Unfortunately, no. They might have all the information we need, but they wouldn't tell me. They wouldn't give me pictures to look at. They wouldn't let me read descriptions of missing people. They kept saying it's all protected by privacy laws. I wanted to tell them your need to know who you are is more important than their damned privacy laws, but I didn't."

The smile that greeted Jack when he looked up a few seconds later was further evidence the man he'd fallen hopelessly in love with over the previous few weeks couldn't possibly be bad in any way, shape, or form. Buddy was the personification of kindness and good-heartedness.

Before he could formulate some wonderful, witty thing to say, Jack found himself with a lap full of his favorite treat—his best friend and all-time favorite man. Thoughts turned away from food for the next hour while other issues took a higher priority.

Chapter Fourteen
Patrick?

WHILE Jack had a job to go to every night to keep his time and his mind occupied, Buddy was not so fortunate. He only occasionally worked at the cannery, so generally he had nothing constructive to do with his time while Jack worked.

At first, he had been so intimidated by the experience of being in a foreign land where he couldn't read the street signs or speak the language that he lived as a hermit in Jack's small house. He occupied himself by doing whatever Jack needed to have done, and he gladly ventured out with Jack, but he was unwilling to do so on his own.

But after several weeks of traipsing about the city with Jack while they searched for clues to his identity and did some sightseeing, Buddy was gaining familiarity with the place. Knowing his way around meant he was willing and able to leave the house to at least run some errands for Jack. When they ran out of something that could be carried home easily while walking, Jack left some money and Buddy went off to buy whatever they needed. There were stores open at all hours of the day or night, so finding places to shop during the night was not a problem.

The first time he successfully managed one of those trips thrilled him to no end. When Jack got home from work after that, Buddy was practically jumping up and down with excitement at what he had done all on his own. Since his friend was so happy, Jack was happy too. He was thrilled to be able to do something to help out for a change.

With a couple of shopping expeditions under his belt, Buddy was willing to go off to check out different things around the city. So long as he knew where he was going and had a plan, he was increasingly willing to venture forth. He felt much more comfortable in the city now he'd seen a lot more of it with Jack.

But one day Buddy got a scare that sent him fleeing from the market he'd been in, running flat-out all the way back to the house in fear. The second Jack stepped through the door that day after work, it was immediately obvious something had happened. Every other day when Jack got home, Buddy always greeted him with a big smile, a hug, and pure delight at having his friend home again.

But that day, Jack had to go hunt for Buddy. And there were simply not many places for anyone to hide in the tiny house they shared. Jack was almost convinced Buddy wasn't home yet from his day of exploring. But then he opened the bathroom door and found the man huddled on the floor hugging himself tightly, rocking gently back and forth.

"Oh my God, what's wrong?" Jack immediately asked, beyond worried about his friend's unusual behavior.

But Buddy remained silent. He simply rocked and tucked his head low.

The bathroom was tiny, even by small-house standards, so it was far from an ideal setting for a conversation. But that was where Buddy was hiding, so that was where Jack had to deal with him and whatever crisis had enveloped his friend.

After much cajoling, Jack was finally able to get the story out of him.

"I was wandering around a small neighborhood near some big hotels by the river. I didn't recognize anything, but I kept having this feeling someone was watching me. But when I stopped and looked around, I didn't see anyone or anything that looked out of order. Then I spotted a man who was staring at me. I moved away from where he was, but he turned up at the next place I went. I tried moving on again, but he followed me again. Each time he got closer to me and started to scare me more and more. Then... then...."

When he hesitated, Jack urged him on. "It's okay. Go on when you're able."

"He spoke to me. But he called me...." Buddy started to say, but then stopped, covering his face with his hands.

"What did he call you?" Jack asked, gently.

"He called me... Patrick."

"Did that name mean anything to you?"

"No," Buddy said, vigorously shaking his head back and forth, one step removed from tears.

"Did he look familiar to you in any way?"

"No."

"How about his voice? Did you recognize the sound of his voice at all?"

"No." Buddy's voice rose in obvious upset.

Jack paused a moment before proceeding, simply kneeling beside his friend and gently rubbing his back, or at least what of it he could reach in such close quarters.

After a few moments had passed in silence, he asked, "What about where you were? Was there anything about the area you were in that seemed familiar in any way?"

"No. Nothing. I didn't recognize him. I didn't know anything about him. I don't know him and I don't know why he wanted me."

"What did you do when you saw him and heard him speak to you?"

"I ran!"

"You ran? Where?"

"Back here, as fast as I could."

"Why? If he knew you, he could be what we've been searching for all these many weeks."

"Because I was scared, Jack," Buddy said, the pitifulness of his feeling obvious in the tone and inflection of his voice.

"I think I understand," Jack said quietly.

"You do?" Buddy finally asked.

"Yes. You were all alone out there. We've been searching for any clue for so long now and have come up empty-handed every step of the way. I can imagine how startling it must have been for some total stranger to stare at you and then speak to you—and for you to understand the language in which he was speaking."

Buddy looked up at Jack, their gazes meeting. "That's right," Buddy said. "I did understand him."

"Was he a non-Thai, like you and me?"

"Yes," Buddy whispered.

"Let's go back. I'll be with you every step of the way. We'll go back and see if he's still there, and I can talk with him for you," Jack volunteered.

"No," Buddy said, vigorously shaking his head.

"This is what we've been looking for all these months. This is the first substantial clue we've found, and we didn't find it. It found us. We have to follow up and see what this is all about."

"Please, Jack. I'm scared," Buddy said.

"I know, mate. But don't be. I'll be there with you."

But Buddy just shook his head vigorously and said, "No."

"Okay. But I'm going to go check it out. Tell me exactly where it was that you saw this guy."

"Please, Jack. Please, don't. I'm scared."

"I'll be very careful. And remember, whoever that guy was, he doesn't have a clue who I am. He's not looking for me. I'm just a face in the crowd."

SO Jack left Buddy, still huddled in the small bathroom— he refused to leave—and headed immediately to the market where Buddy had encountered the man who had apparently recognized him.

Bangkok had more traffic than seemed possible, so getting anywhere during the day was always a relatively slow process. That day, Jack's anxiousness was directly proportional to the congestion on the roads. But finally, forty-five minutes after leaving his house, Jack was at the market where the encounter had apparently taken place.

The market was busy. Thai men and women were seated in stalls, each displaying a wide variety of products, everything from aromatic spices to kitchen utensils, some of which Jack, after living in the country for several years, didn't even recognize. Other markets might have been loud with shouted voices, people hawking their wares, but the Thai were a more gentle people and did not go in for behaviors one might see in the Turkish markets he'd seen years earlier.

Slowly, Jack walked through the relatively small market, smiling and greeting people when appropriate. The market was unusual to Jack in one regard other than the lack of shouting—there were a number of obvious Western tourists in and around the market, most likely from the large tourist hotels nearby.

Jack had come to the market almost directly from the end of his workday. It was only when he smelled something one of the Thai men was cooking in a nearby stall that he realized just how very hungry he was. And in case he didn't notice, his stomach rumbled loudly as a reminder.

Eating from a food stall in the market was easy because there was no menu with multiple options— there was just whatever the owner chose to prepare that day. Jack didn't care what you called it because whatever it was smelled delicious. In short order he had a container of the aromatic chicken and noodle dish and was sitting down at a rickety old metal chair and table to eat. He still found it unusual and a little strange to be eating chicken while another of the creatures walked around near his feet, freely wandering around checking things out. He almost felt the need to apologize for eating one of its cousins, but fought down that urge and kept eating.

Slowly, with his hunger assuaged, Jack sat back and started to study the people coming and going, as well as those who, like him, were seated, eating. It didn't take him long to spot a man who wasn't doing exactly what the others were. This man was sitting quietly watching everyone who came into the area. He was clearly looking for someone, and Jack wanted to know if his suspicions were correct. But before he could get up and make his way the short distance to the man, he got up and came to Jack.

"Excuse me," he said a bit hesitantly. "May I ask you a question?"

"You just did, mate," Jack responded lightly, smiling at the stranger, even though he was a bundle of nerves just beneath the surface.

"So I did. Well, I have a more important question, and I hope you can help me." He pulled a photo from a folder in his hands and passed it to Jack. "Have you seen this man?"

Jack nearly dropped the photo—it was Buddy. He looked happy, but stiff at the same time. And Jack couldn't miss the fatigue that showed in the eyes of the man in the photograph. Jack made a good show of studying the photo for longer than was perhaps necessary.

"Maybe," he said, trying to sound hopeful enough to engage the man in conversation but not so much as to arouse suspicions. "Who wants to know? What's he done? He in some kind of trouble? Is there a reward?" He hoped that last question might throw the questioner off enough to conceal Jack's true feelings.

"No, no, no," the stranger said. "He's not in any trouble. I'm looking for him because he's my brother and he's been missing for months. He came here for work. We know he arrived here, but then he seemed to just vanish. We—our parents and I—are terribly worried. My mother is hopeful, but my father is afraid he might be dead. We can't handle the not knowing, so I'm here searching for him.

"I thought I saw him earlier—well, actually late last night, right here. But he took off as if he'd seen a ghost."

"What's your name, mate?" Jack asked.

"James. My brother's name is Patrick."

"Pull up a chair, James. Sit and talk with me."

Without any additional encouragement, James did precisely as directed.

"You've seen him, haven't you?" James said excitedly. "You know him. You know where I can find him. Please, tell me."

Jack sat and stared intently at the man for several seconds.

"Slow down, mate. I might have seen him around."

"Do you know where I can find him? We are desperate to make sure he's okay."

Jack didn't know quite how to handle this, wishing he was a little less tired than he was. His overnight shift in the factory had been hot and exhausting. But when he'd heard about the potential lead on Buddy's name, he'd immediately left to check it out.

"I've seen him around sometimes. I don't know where he is right now," Jack said, which was technically not a lie.

"Is okay? Is he hurt?"

Breaking eye contact for a moment, Jack quietly considered that question for a moment before he spoke. "He's physically fine," Jack said.

"Physically?" James said, looking panicked. "What's wrong?"

"I'm no doctor, mate. I can't tell you what I don't know. But if the guy I know of is this guy," he said, pointing to the picture in front of him, "I hate to tell you, but he doesn't know…."

"He doesn't know… what?"

"He doesn't remember anything from before he got here. But like I said, that's assuming the guy I know of is the same guy you're after. There's no guarantee they're the same. They could be entirely different men."

"Please," James pleaded. "I am desperate to find him. I know I saw Patrick yesterday, but for some reason he took off, and I couldn't catch him. So I'm begging you, please, if you can help me in any way, any way at all, I will be unbelievably grateful to you."

"Consider what it must be like for someone with no memory to have a stranger trying to corner him," Jack said, taking a chance at tipping his hand. "Can you imagine how that could have scared him?"

"I need to see him. Please!" James pleaded.

"I tell you what," Jack said, feeling somewhat frustrated with James for failing to understand the real situation. "If I see him sometime soon, I can give him a message that you're looking for him and want to talk with him."

The stranger's entire body sagged at that news. "I… thank you, I guess. I hate this… being so close and yet so far."

"If I see him, I'll pass the message on. How can he get hold of you if I do see him? Assuming he's willing to do so."

"I'm staying at the Royal Orchid Sheraton Hotel on the Chao Phraya River."

"Nice," Jack said appreciatively. "That place is expensive, not someplace where anybody would stay for more than a few days."

"I'm here for as long as it takes me to track him down. I hope it doesn't take too long, but finding my brother is more important than anything else."

"Sounds like your family has a bit of money, mate."

"My brother is very important to us. We've all been worried sick about what happened to him. For him to just fall off the face of the earth was so totally out of character for him."

"Had your brother ever been here to Thailand before? Or was this trip his first trip?"

"He came here a couple of times a year for work. He knew the place rather well. He traveled a lot. He didn't think anything of it. Me, on the other hand, I've never been anywhere and can't wait to go home."

Jack snickered, not knowing what else to say.

"How do you know of my brother?" James asked Jack.

"I used to see him around."

"Used to?" James asked.

"I used to see him around quite often, but not so much lately." Okay, he was stretching the truth a little, but he didn't know what else to say. "But I'm sure that if he's still around, I'll be seeing him. You said you'd seen him, what? Last night? Then he's still around. When I see him next, I'll pass your message on." Jack started to get up, but stopped. "Can I get your name and the room number at the Royal Orchid? I know the place, but your brother may not."

"Oh, he knows it quite well. He always stayed there whenever he came to Bangkok."

"Unless he's a man who can't remember who he is," Jack said, frustrated again at James for his failure to understand what he'd told the stranger. "In which case he could have stayed someplace a thousand times before, but that would be meaningless now. Anything from before just doesn't exist for this man."

As he stood up to leave, Jack stopped and turned back. "One question. Does your brother have a girlfriend or boyfriend, husband or wife?"

"No. He was married to his work. He's had a couple of boyfriends, but nothing major. He's single. Can I ask why you want to know?"

Jack smiled. "Just curious. I'll let him know you want to see him and how to find you. Is there a good time of day when you'll be in your room so he can come see you?"

"I'm typically out all morning and then take a break in the afternoon. And then I'm out again late at night when it's a bit less hot. I had no idea this place was so steamy. It takes a lot out of you."

"Tell me about it," Jack said with a smile.

"I'm going to stay here for a few more hours and then go back to my hotel for lunch, and then to my room to take a shower and probably a nap. But if you find Patrick, tell him I don't care what time it is. It can be the middle of the night."

"Will do. I've heard they do a nice high tea each afternoon at your hotel."

"Um, I'll check it out," James said. "You know where he is, don't you? Please, I'm begging you."

"I understand, mate, but you don't know... just let me see what I can do. I make no guarantees, but I promise you I'll try to find him, and if he's willing get him there some afternoon at teatime."

"Thank you. Really, I mean it," James said. "Thank you. The end to this horrible mystery is in sight. Thank you." As Jack turned to leave, though, James called out, "Hey, wait! How can I reach you?"

"Take care, mate," he said as he left to head home, carefully not answering the question James had asked.

He'd walked a couple of blocks before he realized he needed to focus more on how he went about getting home. What if James decided to follow him? What if James had someone else working with him and one of them was following him? Jack was tired, but he was glad he at least thought that through before just dashing directly home.

He could have been home sooner, but because of the convoluted route he took, which included three places where he backtracked, it took him over an hour to get home. He had been tired before he left, but now he was beyond tired. When he finally got home, Jack wanted to take a shower and go to bed.

But the second he was through the door of his house, Buddy was in front of him.

"What happened? Did you learn anything? Did you have trouble? What happened, Jack?" Buddy was close to desperate in his need to know.

Holding up his hands in the universal gesture for stop, Jack said, "One question at a time. I'll give you a quick summary, but I need to get some sleep. I'll tell you every word of it all after I sleep, but yes, I did learn quite a bit. The guy you saw is your brother. His name is James. And you heard correctly—your name is Patrick."

"Patrick. James," he said, as if trying the names on for size. He shook his head slowly. "Doesn't mean anything to me at all. Neither of them. How did you find this out?"

"I talked with him," Jack said.

"How did you find him?" Buddy asked, slightly breathless with anxiety and surprise.

"I just went to where you'd said you'd seen him and he found me."

"How? Why?"

"Because there just aren't all that many white guys around. We kind of stood out. He came over to me and asked me if I'd seen you."

"What did you tell him?"

After Jack filled him in on everything that had been said, including his suggestion they meet at four o'clock for tea one day soon, he lay down.

"Not today, Jack. But I'll think about it. Thank you for going to check it out for me."

"Of course," Jack said as he closed his eyes and drifted off to sleep.

LATER that evening when he opened his eyes, Buddy was right there in front of him, picking up where he'd left off when Jack had fallen asleep. "You'll be there with me, won't you, Jack? I need you there. If you're not there, I'm not going."

"Yes, love, when you're ready, I'll be there with you."

Chapter Fifteen
High Tea

THEY didn't go to high tea at the Sheraton the day Jack met James, but they did go the next afternoon.

Even though they would typically be asleep at that time of day, Jack set an alarm so they could both wake up in time to get ready to leave. With Bangkok traffic, it never hurt to allow a little extra time. Traffic that day was especially brutal and congested, so even with the extra time they'd built in, they only got to the Royal Orchid Hotel with a couple of minutes to spare.

Jack could see that Patrick, as he was trying to start thinking of Buddy, was becoming quite anxious. Moving into an out-of-the-way location in the grand hotel lobby, Jack tried to keep his friend calm. "It's okay. This is a good thing."

"Do you promise?" Patrick asked, only a step or two removed from flat-out panic.

"Yes, I promise," Jack said with a smile. "If I wasn't comfortable with this whole thing, we wouldn't be here. I would never have brought you here if I was at all worried it was bad. I believe we're good. And I'm going to be right beside you. Okay?"

"Okay, Jack. I trust you."

"I know. So, take a deep breath. Hold it for a second, and then slowly let it out. Just relax and let the stress slip away. Okay? I'm right here with you, and I'm going to walk in there with you. And all we're here to do is to meet the guy. You're not going to do anything you're not comfortable with."

Patrick nervously nodded.

"Are we dressed good enough for this place?" Buddy asked him.

"It's what we've got, so it's good enough," Jack said. "You stay here just a minute. I'll go in and take a look, see if he's even in there."

"Okay. Good idea, Jack."

When Jack stepped through the doorway of the famed hotel's restaurant, he almost immediately spotted James, who was seated near the door. It was a question as to who moved faster—the young Thai woman who wanted to seat him, or James. In the end, though, it was James who got to Jack first.

"You're here. Thank goodness. Where is he? Where's my brother?" James anxiously asked.

"Okay, take a breath and calm down," Jack ordered. "He's terrified to meet you, so you've got to get yourself under control. Do you hear me?" Jack demanded politely but firmly. "He's very easily spooked, so you've got to get yourself in hand. If you can't, I should probably just leave so we can try this another day."

Looking pissed, James said, "He's my brother." Finally, though, he agreed. "Fine," he grumbled.

"And lose the attitude. I'm serious. He's very easily spooked by new things."

"I'm not new—" James started to say.

"Yes, you are," Jack said, his impatience showing. "Everything is. Don't you understand anything I've told you?"

"Yes, yes," James said. "Go get him. I'll be over there," he said, gesturing toward the table where he'd been seated when Jack had first come in.

Even though he was having serious second thoughts, Jack returned to the lobby, took Patrick's hand, which was shaking slightly with fear, gave him a hug and a smile, and then led him slowly into the restaurant and toward James's table.

Despite his promises to the contrary, James leapt to his feet on sight of his brother and did exactly the opposite of what Jack had told him.

"Oh my God, Patrick! It's you! It's really you!" James said, wrapping his brother in a hug. "Thank God! Thank God. We've been so worried, so scared, so desperate." When he finally could release his brother, he asked, "What happened? Why didn't you call home? Mom and Dad are freaking out with worry."

Jack could see Patrick was stressing, so he scowled at James and angrily gestured for him to return to his seat while he got Patrick seated and calmed down, whispering softly to him, "It's okay. This is a good thing. Relax."

"Where have you been?" James asked anxiously, with a hint of annoyance in his voice.

"James, take a breath. Don't bombard the poor man with so many questions," Jack ordered him.

"Thanks, Jack," Patrick finally said with a smile. Then he turned to his brother. "I didn't catch your name."

James stared at him for a long moment before he finally understood. "Patrick, it's me, your brother. You know me."

"No, I'm sorry, but I don't. I asked what your name was. If you can't even tell me that, I don't see any reason for us to stay." Patrick moved as if to stand.

"James. I'm your brother, James."

Slowly settling back down into his chair, Patrick said, "Nice to meet you."

"So you can't... you don't... remember?"

"No," Patrick said with a shake of his head. "I'm more... blank, I guess you could say, than anything else." Turning to Jack, he asked, "Can you... could you maybe... I don't know... tell the story. You know, the story we've been able to piece together?"

"Sure," Jack said, giving his friend a reassuring pat on the arm. They all had a much-needed pause while their waiter poured their tea. Turning to James, Jack started to tell the story as he knew it.

"Our best guess is that your brother was involved in a horrific car accident when he arrived in Bangkok. As near as we can tell, he was in a cab when another vehicle, probably a truck but we're not sure, hit them. As we've pieced the story together from third- and fourth-hand accounts, his cab was hit by a couple of other cars and another truck, which tore it apart and sent most of it careening off the road and down an embankment. It rolled over who knows how many times before it came to rest next to the river, where it exploded less than a minute later."

James gasped in obvious horror, but did not interrupt Jack's recitation of the story.

"The driver was killed in the crash, but your brother, Patrick, was somehow able to get out of the car. But when I found him a couple of days later, he was a mess."

Jack described the condition of Patrick's clothes, how tattered and charred they were. He also told James about how he and Patrick met.

"Jack saved my life," Patrick said.

"When I found him, he had no memory, he had no identification on him, no money of any sort, and he was desperately hungry. The poor man was a stranger in what to him was a very strange land. He was eating whatever he could scavenge off the ground near a factory."

"Don't forget how I robbed Boon Tan," Patrick said with a chuckle. "It took me weeks of work to get her to believe I was sincere when I apologized." Now he was able to laugh, since he and Boon Tan had become more friendly. But he clearly remembered their first encounter.

"What?" James gasped. "You stole… you robbed somebody?"

"I was starving, and she had a great big tomato growing in her front yard. I'm sorry, but yes, I stole it. But don't worry," Patrick said. "She got even. The woman has a wicked pitching arm on her. I can still almost feel where she hit me with that pineapple."

Jack joined him in laughter at the memory. "Once you made friends with her, everyone accepted you in our little neighborhood. You charmed them all by helping anytime someone needed something done."

"I was glad to do it. Everyone was so nice to me."

Jack picked up the story again to explain more of it to James. "He hid during the daytime, but at night, when it was dark, he came out and picked up stray pineapples. It took a while, but I finally lured him out of his hiding place with food and water."

Patrick unexpectedly jumped in at that point. "He took me in. He fed me and gave me a place to sleep. He didn't have much, but he gladly shared everything with me even though he didn't know me. I… I owe him everything.

"But I don't know anything. I don't recognize you. I don't know that name you called me. It's all… just blank. I can almost, maybe kind of remember the crash, the fire, the explosion. I do remember running and running and running, feeling terrified that I had to get away from something. I knew I needed to get away from something or someone; it turned out to be the fire. That's the first thing I remember."

"Oh, Patrick, I'm so sorry. But thank God we've finally found you now. And Jack, thank you. I don't know if I'm happy with you or furious with you. When we talked earlier, you knew where he was, didn't you?"

"I did. But it was up to him what happened next. Not me. I couldn't decide for him. So I went back after we talked and told him everything you'd said to me."

James had an iPad in front of him. He turned it on, flipped through a couple of screens, and then turned it toward Patrick and Jack.

"That's us," James said. "You, me, Mom, and Dad, taken last Christmas." When no flicker of recognition passed over his face, James moved on to some other photos. "Here we are skiing in Colorado. Here's you and Mom when you were a little boy. And then you and Dad when you were about the same age."

James flipped to another photo and smiled. "And this one, I love this one, this one is you holding me right after Mom and Dad brought me home from the hospital. My big brother had me and took care of me. We love you, Patrick. I'm here to take you home so we can get some medical care for you and help you get your memories back.

"There's some great neurologists back in the US. You need to see them and see what they can do to help you. The sooner the better."

Patrick looked at James and said simply, "No. I live here. I don't want to go anywhere else, especially some place I don't know and where I don't know anybody. The place sounds so foreign to me. My entire life is here. Everyone I know is here. I'm happy here."

"Patrick, you live in the US. I'm here to take you back home."

"No," Patrick shouted, standing up from the table as the other guests in the room turned their way to see who was shouting and why. "Come on, Jack, let's go home."

"Just a minute," Jack said, but Patrick was already walking away.

"You really need to learn to back the fuck off, mate," Jack said to James as he stood up to follow his friend. He threw the linen napkin onto the table with a disgusted shake of his head for James.

"Where are you going?" James demanded.

"I told you not to scare him, but that's exactly what you had to do, wasn't it?" Jack demanded, pissed off at James.

Jack left to follow Patrick, but unfortunately James was right on his heels.

Patrick was pacing outside the front entrance of the hotel. "Let's go, Jack," he said when Jack caught up with him.

"Please!" James pleaded. "I'm sorry, Patrick. I still think of the Patrick I've always known."

"I don't know him," Patrick said simply.

"Patrick, I'm sorry I forgot you don't remember any of that. I'm sorry I scared you. I didn't mean to."

Patrick scowled at him and repeated, "Come on, Jack."

Jack shook hands with James and said, "It was nice meeting you, James. Have a good trip home."

"I'm not going anywhere," James told them both, puffing his chest out and straightening his back to look authoritative. "We're not finished. I can't go anywhere yet."

"Yes, we are," Patrick said. "Your brother is dead. Let him rest in peace."

But unfortunately James followed them as Patrick led the way away from the hotel. "Please, Pat, I'm sorry. I didn't mean to push you too fast. This is all new for me, and it's a huge change. Please be patient with me. I don't mean to scare you. We've just been so terribly worried about you, not knowing where you were, if you were dead or alive. It is so incredible to finally find you."

Patrick stopped and looked back at James. "You found me, now go home and tell whoever you want, but leave me alone."

"I can't do that. I have to stay here."

"Why?"

"If I went home now without you, Mom and Dad would never forgive me."

"Then why aren't they here?" Patrick asked the obvious.

"You know Mom has never—"

"I don't know anything! Haven't you been listening to anything we've said?" Patrick practically screamed at his brother. He stopped, took a deep breath, closed his eyes, and slowly exhaled, trying to get himself back under control.

"You're right. I did it again. I'm sorry," James said. "I cannot leave until I have convinced you to come back to the US with me so we can get medical care for you."

Patrick fell silent, staring at him for the longest time. "I'll think about it," he finally said, surprising both Jack and James. "Now go back to your hotel. If I want to find you, I know where you are."

"Where can I find you?" James asked.

"You can't," Patrick said with supreme authority that conveyed his desired message. "Don't call me— I'll call you."

Jack was so surprised to see this side of Patrick. Surprised and a bit aroused as well, truth be told.

James didn't argue, but did ask, "Can we get together again?"

Jack took a chance and joined the conversation. "How about dinner in a couple of nights?"

"Sure. Anything," James agreed.

"Patrick?" Jack asked, still finding it odd to use this name for his lover.

"Fine," he said, clearly unhappy but also understanding this was something they needed to do.

"How about Tuesday night, seven o'clock, back here at your hotel restaurant?" Jack suggested, immediately taking the lead.

"Why not tomorrow?" James pushed.

"Because we have a lot to talk about and think about," Jack said without hesitation. "I think your brother has already shown you that pushing him too far, too fast will only backfire on you and do exactly the opposite of what you intend."

It was obvious James wanted to argue, but to Jack's surprise, he did not. Instead, he nodded. "All right, Tuesday evening at seven o'clock would be great. I look forward to seeing you back here then."

With several glances of deep suspicion over his shoulder as they walked away, Patrick led them quickly away from the hotel. Jack didn't argue or resist, knowing Patrick needed to put some distance between himself and his brother so he could begin to process all this new information.

TUESDAY evening they showed up at the hotel a few minutes past seven. It had been a struggle for Jack to get Patrick there at all, but he'd finally consented and come along reluctantly.

"Gentlemen, welcome," James greeted them with an attempt at cheerfulness. Jack was impressed James remained seated, instead just extending his arm to shake hands with both of his guests.

Once everyone was seated, James asked Jack, "Is it always this hot here?"

"At this time of year, you can count on heat and humidity. If you think this is bad, try coming here during the monsoon season, when it rains for days on end."

"I think I'll pass on that, actually," James said, laughing. "Thank you for coming to dinner. I hope the traffic wasn't too bad for you, getting here from wherever you had to come."

Patrick surprised Jack by taking that one himself. "The traffic always seems congested here in Bangkok. I can't recall ever seeing the roads wide open."

"That's because it hasn't happened in twenty years or so," Jack joked, all of them sharing a laugh that helped to lighten their moods.

Jack expected James to launch into his pitch again, but was pleasantly surprised he did not. Through their perusal of the menu, ordering, dining, James didn't push Patrick. It was only after dinner as they were having coffee and tea that he brought the subject up.

"Have you had some time to think about what I mentioned last time we were together?"

"You mean me going with you to wherever you live?" Patrick asked.

"Yes," James said.

"Yes," Patrick replied.

"Can I answer any questions for you?" James offered.

"Where do you live?" Jack asked.

"I live in Los Angeles, which is in California on the west coast of the United States."

"How far is that?" Patrick asked.

"Several thousand miles. I'm not sure exactly how far it is."

"So, it takes a while to fly there?" Patrick asked.

"Yes, the better part of a day," James responded.

"I don't have any money," Patrick volunteered, "so if you have to pay to fly, I can't go anywhere."

"That's not a problem," James said. "You have worked hard all your life and have amassed some savings. But don't worry. Our father will cover the cost of you flying back to Los Angeles."

"Why?" Patrick asked.

"He's your father. He's been devastated at the thought of losing you."

"Why? He's got you," Patrick said.

James snickered. "You and Dad have always been closer because the two of you are so much alike. I'm more like our mother, although if you ever ask me to confirm that I admitted it, I'll deny all knowledge of this conversation."

Jack laughed, and while Patrick didn't really understand what his brother was saying, he followed Jack's lead and smiled with them.

"Dad built his own company and ran it for years," James explained. "He's retired now, so money is not an issue for him and Mom. They are very comfortable financially. But to answer your earlier question, he was concerned about trying to make this trip and search for you on his own because he's not as young as he used to be. That's why he asked me to come in his place."

"And your mother?" Patrick asked. "Is she aged as well?"

"Don't ever tell her I said so. But the real reason is because she has never left the country and doesn't want to do so now. She's very happy living within a few miles of where she was born. She's scared of the big, bad world, and her way around that is just to stay home and let us go off as we need to."

Patrick nodded. "I don't have any documents I would need to be able to travel," Patrick said. "Jack told me that you need some kind of little book—"

"Passport," Jack said.

"That's it, a passport that proves who I am. I don't have anything like that. If I ever did, it was destroyed in that accident Jack was describing to you the last time we met."

Both Patrick and Jack watched as James reached into his jacket pocket and pulled out something, which he slid across the table to his brother.

"Dad pulled some strings and got them to issue a replacement passport for you so you can travel."

Patrick sat and slowly stroked the passport, running his fingers over the thick material of the cover, feeling the lettering. He finally opened it and flipped one by one through the pages. Stopping at the page that identified him, he smiled and pointed at the photo. "That's me," he said, smiling at Jack while holding it up for him to see.

"Yep," Jack agreed, looking over his partner's shoulder. "That's you, Buddy," Jack slipped and used his old name for Patrick.

They all sat quietly for a moment as Patrick read the words and considered what they said about who he was.

"You don't approve of me being with Jack," Patrick said suddenly.

"Jack seems like a great guy. And it sounds like he's saved your life. I'm very grateful to him."

"Then why do you want to take me away from Jack?" Patrick asked. "Why do you want to separate us?"

"I just want to get medical attention for you," James said.

"This place is all I know. I don't know anything but here and now."

"I'm hopeful if you can get to see a good neurologist, they might be able to help you recover what you've lost."

He mulled over the words his brother was speaking. Even though he didn't want to confirm what James was saying, he had to admit he wanted deep down to know who he had been. But the big problem with that was he was so very happy with Jack. Jack had done so much for him. Jack had rescued him, saved him. He owed

Jack everything. But did he owe Jack his past if there was some way to remember who he had been?

"But I like who I am now," Patrick said.

The three of them were quiet, each deep in thought.

"Remembering who you were before doesn't mean you lose who you are here," Jack said. "I'm no doctor, but I don't think your old memories would wipe out your new memories, only add to them. You'd still know me, but you'd know who you were before you came here."

"If anything can be done for me," Patrick added. "It's been months since the accident. Nothing has changed in all that time. We've worked so hard to find out what happened to me."

"Did you go to the embassy?" James asked.

"No!" Patrick answered immediately.

"I don't understand."

"Like I told you, my very first memory here was of running from something or someone. I didn't know what. I was scared maybe someone was after me and wanted to hurt me. Jack went but they wouldn't tell him anything."

Since they hadn't talked about it before, Patrick filled his brother in on some of their efforts to recover his memories, including Jack's abortive trip to the American Embassy.

"Please, Pat," James pleaded. "Come home with me. Mom and Dad are frantic with worry. Dad was convinced you were dead, but Mom still had hope even though it had been months with no word. They are going to be so happy to have you back home."

"But…," Patrick started and turned to look at Jack before turning back to his brother. "This is home."

"No, Pat, your home is a very long ways away from here."

"But this is the only home I've ever known. I don't want to leave it. Jack, I can't," Patrick said, sounding panicked.

"It's okay. You can do it, babe. You're strong. Look at everything you've gone through and how you've survived. You are the strongest man I know."

"You're coming with me, aren't you, Jack?" Patrick asked.

Jack had been dreading this question. "I'm afraid I can't. I have to work. If I don't work at the cannery, I have to give up my house, since they are for workers at the plant. Also, I can't leave Thailand. My passport has expired. So I'm afraid I can't go on this trip with you. And besides, I could never afford the price of flying to the United States. Remember, I'm just a poor guy working in a pineapple cannery and living in a falling-down little house."

"It's not falling down," Patrick complained forcefully. "It's beautiful. You've done so much work to make it strong and comfortable and efficient. It's home." Patrick looked down without saying a word. The other two let him have his time to think. "What should I do, Jack?"

"I can't decide that for you," Jack said. "But I think it makes sense for you to go with your brother now to see your parents and to see the doctors he talked about. Hopefully they can help you remember what you've lost."

It pained Jack so much to say those words. He didn't want Patrick to leave. He feared if Patrick left he'd never come back. But Jack knew if there was any hope of Patrick recovering who he'd once been, they had to give it a shot.

"And after you've done all that," Jack went on, "you know right where I am. I'm not going anywhere. There's nothing that says you can't come back and see me after you go with him now."

He smiled at Patrick, fighting to keep back the tears. Losing his best friend, his lover, the man who'd brightened up his life, was sheer torture for Jack. But he knew it was the only option. Patrick needed to be with his family. Hopefully being with them, surrounded by everything he'd known, would help him to remember. But what could possibly come after that was anybody's guess.

"When… when would you… you know, when are you leaving here?" Jack asked James.

"I only came here to find Patrick," James said decisively. "I've found him, so I'm ready to go as soon as I can get two seats on the next available flight."

"I… so you could… I mean… you could get that set up when? Like tomorrow? The next day? For sometime later, like this week, next week?"

"If Patrick's willing to go with me, I can call my assistant right now and get it booked. Is that okay with you?" James addressed his question to Patrick. He was learning how to work with his brother.

"Why don't you make whatever calls you need to, and Jack and I can come back tomorrow night for dinner again," Patrick suggested. "It's getting late, and Jack needs to get to work."

"You work nights?" James asked, getting a nod of affirmation from both men.

"Patrick, you could stay here at the hotel with me tonight so we can get everything set up."

"No," Patrick said immediately and decisively. There was no question on how he viewed that idea.

"Like I was describing to you before, I'm like our mother in that I hate to be away from home. And I've been away from home a long time. I want to go home, Pat, and I can't do that until you go home with me. Please."

Patrick sat silently, trying to decide what to do.

"Pat, before you two leave, do you have time enough to come upstairs to my room for a few minutes?"

Patrick looked at Jack, who nodded once.

"Okay," Patrick said. "But why?"

"I need to make a quick phone call," James said.

Without further discussion, the three men left the dining room and moved upstairs to a lovely room with an incredible view of the river far below. James busied himself with making a phone call before surprising Patrick by holding his cell phone out to him.

"What?" Patrick asked, confused.

"It's for you."

"I don't know anybody."

"Take the call," James said with a smile. "It's a good thing."

Reluctantly, Patrick took the telephone and cautiously moved it toward his ear, almost as if he was afraid the thing was going to bite him.

"Hello?" he said hesitantly.

"Son? Is that you? Oh, thank goodness. You're alive. Please, son, come home to us. Your father and I have been so worried these last few months. Are you okay?"

The woman on the other end of the call spoke so much and so quickly that Patrick had a few seconds to collect himself before he was expected to speak. When the break came, his question was simple.

"Who is this?"

"Patrick. It's me. It's your mother. Don't you recognize my voice, baby?"

"No. I'm sorry. I don't remember anything. All I know is here, which is my home."

"No, son, please. You've got to come home so we can get you the medical attention you need."

"I told this man here, this James person, that I would consider it. But I am scared to leave everything I know to go off with someone I don't know to a place I don't know. I'm only now getting comfortable with my life here."

"But this is your home, son. We want to bring you home. We love you, baby," his mother wept. "Please, I need you to come home."

Patrick heard her emotion clearly in the call, but it had less impact on him than it would have if he could remember the woman who was speaking to him.

"As I told James, I am considering it, and I do not appreciate being bullied into deciding to do something I'm not ready to do. I need to think about it and talk it over with Jack."

"Who's Jack?" his mother asked.

"He saved my life. I wouldn't be here if it wasn't for Jack. I owe him everything. He took me in, fed me, clothed me, gave me shelter, took care of me. I feel safe with him."

"Bring him with you," his mother said.

"I wish I could, but we can't do that."

"Your father has a lot of political connections. Maybe he could make some calls and work it out, whatever the problem might be."

"Thank you for your kind offer. I'll discuss it with Jack."

Without a farewell, he simply thrust the phone back toward James, who took it and left the room to continue the conversation with their mother.

Patrick had been leaning heavily toward going with James, but the phone call made him reconsider everything.

"Why did you do that to me?" Patrick demanded of his brother when James reentered the room, a move that clearly surprised James.

"I wanted you to talk with Mom and Dad."

"Why? I don't know them. You know that," Patrick said.

"We thought maybe if you heard their voices you'd remember something. Nothing?"

"No. If I go with you, you need to get her to back off. She was... overwhelming."

James chuckled. "She can be that way sometimes. Especially when she's trying to protect her family."

"Jack, what should I do? I'm so confused," Patrick said, shaking his head back and forth in frustration.

Patrick gripped Jack's hand and turned plaintive eyes toward him.

"It's okay," Jack told him. "I think it's a good thing. It's okay. They're your family, and it really seems like they want to help you."

"I... I know," Patrick said. "But I hate the idea of leaving you. That woman said her husband could make some calls and try to work out something so you could go with me."

Jack smiled and said softly, "It's not that simple, I'm afraid."

Patrick had much to consider. He needed to move around a bit, so he stood and moved to the window, his hands thrust into his pants pockets, trying to take in the incredible view from the huge windows of the room they were in. He had never seen the city from this vantage point. It was quite different than living on the ground in the midst of the chaos.

James cast a questioning look at Patrick and then Jack.

"He's thinking," Jack said softly. James nodded in understanding and remained silent, taking a seat across from Jack.

"If I do this, you'll be here... you know, when I get back?" Patrick asked suddenly of Jack, stepping back to him. "You won't go anywhere?"

"I'll be right where I have been. If you want to come back for any reason, I'll be right here waiting for you. You'll always have a place here with me. I promise. Okay?"

"Why wouldn't I want to come back here? This is home. You are home, Jack. I... you're all the life I know. You're all the life I need or could possibly want."

Turning to James, he said, "You need to get that woman on the telephone to not crowd me too much. I get the impression she's a stubborn person who doesn't like things to not work out the way she wants. She talked a lot. It was too much to try to take in. She needs to back off. Can you do that?"

"I'll try. But she's your mother, and she's been living in fear for you for months. She's so grateful you're alive. She's overjoyed by the news. She's going to be so happy to see you and hug you and hold you tight."

Patrick looked away before saying, "She has to not crowd me. It was scary when you acted like you knew me. That's not a 'me' I recognize. You were trying to hug someone I'm not."

"I think I understand," James said softly. "I'll be with you. Every step of the way. That's what brothers do for one another. I promise that before this happened, we were the best of friends and we always looked out for one another. I'm happy you're back too. And I promise to not abandon you but to stick close as you make this journey."

With so much to consider, Patrick returned to the window for a moment to look at everything and nothing. He felt Jack behind him and smiled when he felt Jack's arms encircle his waist and simply hold him.

"You can do it," Jack whispered. "You're the strongest man I know."

"I'm not strong," Patrick protested, wrapping his arms around himself on top of Jack's.

"Oh, yeah?" Jack said. "When you found yourself in a horrible situation, hurt, injured, alone, lost, you found shelter, you found food, you took care of yourself very skillfully. You, my friend, are a very strong man. You can do this. And if it doesn't work, you come back here. I will be right here waiting for you as if you never went anywhere."

Patrick nodded, turned to James, and said, "Are those people going to try to hold me there against my will, as their prisoner? I need your assurance that I will be able to leave if I want to. I... I want that promise. If you can do that for me, I... I will go with you."

Smiling, James said, "I understand, and absolutely, I promise. I'll go call my assistant right now and see when we can leave."

James returned about fifteen minutes later.

"We can leave here tomorrow afternoon," he said with a huge smile. "There are a couple of options. We can fly from here to Tokyo, where we change planes and then proceed on to LA. Or we can fly from here to Hong Kong. The Tokyo option means a little longer first leg."

Patrick looked all around, the equivalent of pacing. He didn't know what to do. What did he know about things like Tokyo or Hong Kong? He'd never heard of places like that. How was he supposed to help? He couldn't, and that frustrated the hell out of him.

Finally, though, his mind was made up.

"I'll go with you tomorrow, but only if you can guarantee, if you can promise me I can come back here. I'm not going to be held there against my will, and I am not going to go there forever. I want you to promise me that you can get me back here after I've been at your home to see these doctors you talk about. Can you do that?" Patrick knew he was repeating his demand, but he wanted to make sure he and James were clear on that point.

"Yes. I can do that," James readily agreed again.

Patrick suspected that James would have agreed to just about anything right then, whether he meant it or not. All he could do at the moment was to hope James would keep his word.

"Say it," Patrick ordered sharply.

"I'll help you get back here after you've traveled with me to Los Angeles to try to get your memory back."

Patrick looked at Jack, who just nodded sadly at him.

"All right. What time should I be back here tomorrow?"

"We'll need to leave here about nine o'clock in the morning to head to the airport."

Again, Patrick looked at Jack before agreeing. "We'll be here. I want you to write down my name, the address where you're taking me, and how to reach me there. I want that for Jack before I will go anywhere. I want him to know where I'm going, where you're taking me."

"Of course," James said, grabbing a hotel pad and writing down everything his brother had requested.

"It will be okay, babe," Jack reassured him. "It sounds like your people have some money and can get you the help you need to remember everything."

"I don't care who they are or what they have. You're all I need, Jack, and I don't want to lose what we've had."

"You won't. You'll get your old memories back and just integrate the old stuff with everything we've done together. You're never gonna get rid of me," Jack said, squeezing Patrick's hand. He leaned forward and gave his lover a kiss, not a quick peck on the cheek, but a kiss that said "I love you" and so much more.

JACK and Patrick left the Sheraton that evening and walked home, both wrapped up in their own thoughts but comforted by the presence of the other beside him. Occasionally their arms bumped into one another as they walked, but they remained silent.

Practically the moment they got back, Jack had to head to work. "I really hate having to leave you," Jack said. "I'll see if I can get out early so we can have some time together before you have to leave."

Patrick nodded, giving Jack a bone-crushing hug before he left to head to work.

IN the morning, Patrick and Jack met James in the hotel lobby at the agreed-upon time.

"Here," James said, holding out several shopping bags for Patrick. "I bought some more appropriate clothes for you for travel. You should change before we leave."

Jack accompanied Patrick to the bathroom to help him get dressed in the new clothing. When they returned to the lobby, though, it was time for Patrick and James to leave for the airport.

"Okay, our car is ready. We should go," James said gently.

Patrick and Jack had had their farewell earlier, so now they just grabbed on to each other and held, gently rocking back and forth, silent.

James interrupted to say, "We need to leave." Turning to Jack, he said, "Thank you so much, Jack. We owe you more than we can ever possibly repay. You saved our lost sheep. Thank you so much."

James tried to slip Jack an envelope of cash, but when he saw what it was, Jack thrust it back at him. "I don't want your money, mate. Just take care of him."

"I will, but please, take this," James insisted.

Gripping and holding tight to James's hand, Jack spoke with deadly seriousness. "Just take care of him. I'm trusting you, mate. Don't let me down."

As James got into the car, Patrick hugged Jack with an intensity that was almost painful. "I'm going to miss you. Are you sure you can't come with us?"

"Yes, I'm sure. But I'll be right here waiting if you want to come back."

"*When*, Jack… not if. When. Am I doing the right thing?" Patrick asked him, a look of sheer panic on his face.

Even though it was happening so fast and Jack was anything but happy, he put on the best brave front he could and said, "I believe you're doing the right thing. And remember, when you're ready, you know you've got me here waiting for you."

"Thanks, Jack, for everything. For taking me in when I was such a total basket case. For everything. You're the best friend I've ever had. I'm going to come back as soon as I can."

He gave Patrick a quick kiss on the lips and said, "Travel safe, my love."

"See you soon," Patrick said.

He slipped into the back seat of the town car beside his brother, the bellman immediately closing the door behind him. As Jack watched the car pull away, he felt like a part of himself was being taken away, and he felt like he was about to crumble to pieces right where he stood.

Chapter Sixteen
Jack

THE walk back to his house that morning was a long, sad trek for Jack. He shouldn't have walked. It was too far. It was too damned hot and humid in the full sun of another sweltering day in Thailand. But Jack needed to walk; he needed the physical activity. He needed the motion. He needed to dodge around cars stuck in rush hour traffic. He needed to be doing something. He needed to overload his senses with anything other than the weight of his overwhelming grief. He needed the noise of the vehicles and the people everywhere around him. He needed the stench of the car and truck exhaust, the odors of gas, the smell of the river. He could not sit in the back of a cab and do nothing. Activity, doing something, things that overloaded his senses—those were the things that saved Jack from totally falling apart that morning. He knew it was likely to happen sometime soon, but he couldn't do it right then. Not yet. It was too raw; it would hurt too much. He needed some time to toughen himself up before that happened.

When they'd parted, he'd told Patrick what Patrick needed to hear, but it wasn't what Jack wanted to do. It wasn't what Jack needed to hear. What he'd wanted was to tell Patrick not to go, to stay right where he was, that they would get through it together. He loved Patrick, and now the thought of being separated from him for who knew how long, perhaps forever, was just torture for him. There were no guarantees Patrick would ever come back.

For all Jack knew, Patrick would see some doctors, some specialists back in the United States, and they would fix him with their first-world medical technology so he could remember everything. They would unlock all his memories. And he so desperately feared Patrick would look at his time with Jack and wonder how the hell he could have been so stupid, so crazy as to get involved with someone like Jack.

When Patrick had asked about losing what he'd known there in Bangkok, Jack had been brave and told him his old memories would just be layered on top of his existing memories from Thailand. But what did he know? He was no brain doc. For all he knew, when they got inside his head and started messing around, the man he'd known could just disappear. And with him would go the best friend and lover Jack had ever known.

And Jack hurt. There was just no way around it. Jack hurt. When he finally reached home, he was exhausted, which was perfect. What wasn't perfect was that he wanted to take a shower before he lay down to sleep, but there wasn't enough water, so the only option he had was to strip off his clothes and use a minimal amount of warm water to wipe himself down at the sink.

Usually when he lay down to sleep, the heat didn't bother him much. But it did that day. Maybe it was because he was going to bed later than usual, in the hottest part of the day. Whatever it was, Jack could not settle down, could not get comfortable, and most definitely could not fall asleep. First he tossed one way, sweating on his left side. Then he'd roll over to the other side and sweat there. His legs became tangled up in the sheets as they became soaked with sweat.

Jack was a miserable man. He tried getting out of bed to get something to eat, but he had no appetite, so he lay back down. He did manage to fall asleep that time, but when his alarm went off, telling him it was time to head to work, Jack was unhappy and grumpy. Too little sleep was almost worse than no sleep at all. But he had no choice. Jack had to get ready.

Even though he had no appetite, Jack fixed something simple for his dinner and forced himself to leave his little house and all its reminders of his missing lover and make his way over to the cannery.

Work that night was both good and bad. It was good in that he was especially busy, but it was bad in that he was totally exhausted, emotionally, mentally, and physically. But he had to work. People didn't just give you money. You had to work to get money, and you needed money to do anything in this world.

Hour after hour he watched tens of thousands of pineapples being peeled, cored, and canned. The husks that were left after they'd been squeezed for their juice were picked up by farmers who used them for hog feed. Who knew pigs had a taste for sweet pineapple. The factory was old, very old, but all the equipment still worked, so they still processed pineapples just as workers had there for untold decades.

Between the trucks coming in to bring more pineapples from the fields and the trucks going out with the packed, sealed, labeled, and boxed cans of pineapple fruit and pineapple juice, there was nonstop activity at their small plant.

At the end of his shift, Jack made his way back to his house and crawled into bed, exhausted from all his walking the previous day followed by working a full shift in the factory. They hadn't had rain in a couple of days, so there still wasn't enough water for a shower. He was hopeful they'd get rain soon to replenish his supply. He desperately wanted to take a shower, but there was barely enough to wash his hands and his face.

When Patrick had come to live with him, Jack had made some modifications to his rainwater collection system to double its capacity and capture twice as much as before. Even so, without rain he couldn't take a shower.

As he lay in bed, he couldn't help but think of Patrick. If his flight had taken off from Bangkok on time, he'd already be a long, long ways away and getting farther away from him with every second. For all Jack knew, he could be in Los Angeles by now.

Jack couldn't remember how long the flight was, but he remembered it was a long, long trip. He hadn't thought to ask James for the layovers on the flights they were on. The internet might exist out in the rest of the world, but it didn't exist where he lived. Maybe he could ask a friend in the factory offices to let him use their computer to look up the details. But that would mean getting up out of bed and getting dressed again. And Jack didn't want to do that. His mind wouldn't let him shut down and go to sleep, but he was at least comfortable lying down. So he stayed put. And eventually he fell into a restless sleep.

Chapter Seventeen
Patrick

DURING the ride to the airport, Patrick had second, third, and fourth doubts, with many more beyond that. Every tenth of a mile they traveled, with every click of the taxi meter, he considered telling James he couldn't do this, he had to go back, he wanted to go back to Jack.

Every time the car slowed down due to traffic congestion, he wanted to throw the door open and jump from the car, making a break for it. But he didn't. He kept his doubts pressed down deep inside, right next to his fear, which was close to overwhelming. The two elements combined to make him almost jittery enough to jump out of his skin. He was so anxious that at one stage of the departure formalities, an officer had asked him, "Are you all right, sir?"

"What? Oh, sorry. Yes. I've never flown before," Patrick said. He probably had, but he didn't remember those flights. The officers seemed to regard him with increased suspicion, so he amended his answer. "Sorry, I'm nervous flying. I hate flying." That appeared to work, and the officer waved him through.

He didn't have a clue how he felt about flying, but he was about to find out the hard way. He hoped it wasn't a problem for him. Oh, great, one more thing to be anxious and worried about.

"Pat," James said softly to him once they cleared that checkpoint. "Would you like some mild antianxiety medication? I always carry some with me. They don't knock you out; they just sort of make the anxiousness less of an issue. I hate to travel, like I said. I especially hate to fly, so I always take one before I get on an airplane. Then I take another one or two once we're on our way. I guess I'm happy if I can just get so mellow I fall asleep and wake up when it's almost over. Never quite works that way, but I can dream anyway," he said with a smile.

When Patrick hesitated, James gave him an example of how they worked.

"Here, I'll take one right now. You can watch me and see how it affects me and then decide for yourself. How does that sound?"

"Sure. Fine. Anything."

James took his pill with water from a bottle he'd purchased after they cleared the final ring of security. Things had moved relatively smoothly for them so far that morning, so they were well ahead of schedule. They'd already purchased a couple of paperback books to read during the flight. All that was left now was to walk, because soon they would start their marathon of being seated.

For the next hour they walked from one end of the terminal to the other and back again, over and over again.

"Feeling more calm now we're through all that front-end clearance stuff?" James asked.

"Oh, that didn't bother me. I'm just…."

"Still not sure you've made the right decision," James said, surprising his brother by figuring out what was really going on with him. "I know. You are making the right choice. And like I said, I'm here with you each step of the way. And you're just going to the United States for a visit. Think of it that way. You're going to go the US, see some doctors, visit some family, and then when you're ready, you leave and come back here if that's what you want to do. We will miss you, but I think now I understand. It will take Mom and Dad a lot longer to get to that point. I guess it's always tough for parents."

"Do you have children?" Patrick asked, suddenly realizing he knew next to nothing about the man he was traveling with.

"I do. I have a son and a daughter. They're ten and eight."

"You miss them?" Patrick asked.

"Of course."

"Why did you leave them to come over here?" Patrick asked.

"Because you're my brother and you were lost. We're family. You'd have done the same for me if our roles were reversed."

Patrick didn't say anything. He didn't know that he would, because he still didn't know who he was. For months now he'd struggled, wrestled with his blasted mind, trying to shake loose something, a thread of a memory, a wisp of a memory, anything that might help him to have even a glimpse of who he was.

But every single time he'd tried, those efforts had all ended the same way, in complete and total failure. No matter how he went about it, Patrick's memories remained as missing in action as they had been when this whole mess started.

"We need to head to our gate," James said, pulling him back to the present.

"Is it… is it time?"

"Yes," he said, smiling gently at his anxious brother.

"Okay." They were close, so they didn't have to go far. As they stood, waiting for boarding to start, Patrick turned to James and asked, "Will I be allowed to meet your family?"

"Of course, Patrick. Why wouldn't you?"

"Do they know me?"

"My kids? Yes, of course they do. They've missed you too. We all have."

"Tell me about where we live," Patrick asked suddenly.

"Well, we live in the Los Angeles area in Southern California. It's a huge metropolitan area with millions of people and lots of traffic."

"Like Bangkok?"

"In that regard, yes, very much so," James said with a chuckle. "But cleaner." Further discussion had to wait, though, as their cabin was called for boarding. Leading Patrick to a separate doorway, they boarded with a smaller group of people than the large group standing off to the right awaiting boarding elsewhere on the airplane.

As they stepped aboard the jumbo jet that was prepared to carry them all the way across the ocean to the unknown, Patrick looked around and was impressed with the roominess of the cabin where their seats were located.

"I thought it would be more claustrophobic than this," Patrick observed. "This is quite... nice."

"This is the first-class cabin," James explained. "These seats are the nicest, but also the most costly. Behind us is the business-class cabin, where the seats are a bit tighter. And then beyond that is the economy cabin, or coach, where the seats are most tightly packed together. Those seats are typically the cheapest."

"Why aren't we seated back there?"

"Because our father sprang for the cost of these seats, and because I'd rather roll around naked over hot coals and broken glass than sit back there for a sixteen-plus-hour flight when the plane is full like it is today. You've done it a lot more than I have. You've always amazed me by being willing to do that."

"How different are the prices between there and here?" Patrick asked.

"Um, let me see," James said. "With the money for each of our seats, you could probably buy ten tickets in the coach cabin."

"That's a major difference," Patrick observed.

Chapter Eighteen
Home?

AS soon as their jumbo jet was in the air at the start of their very long trip back to the United States, they both ate the meal provided, but while James lay back and went to sleep, Patrick remained wide-awake. Just when Patrick could have used his comfort, his reassurance, a simple conversation, James wasn't available.

He knew James hated to fly. They'd had that conversation. So he knew sleeping was the way James coped with the anxiety of a long flight. This left Patrick with lots of uninterrupted time to rethink what he'd agreed to do. If he could have gotten off the plane and gone back to Jack, he would have done that several dozen times during the first hour of the flight.

There was no direct flight available from Bangkok all the way to Los Angeles, so James had booked them on a flight that had one stopover in Hong Kong. But the same plane would continue onward to the United States, so there was no need for them to get off the plane or change planes. Still, they would be on the ground for a couple of hours.

The flight from Bangkok to Hong Kong was a relative short two hours and twenty minutes. Patrick woke James when they were about to land, and got him upright for the landing in Hong Kong.

They picked up some new passengers, but those in first class, where James and Patrick were seated, remained largely the same. Every seat in the small cabin at the front of the plane was filled once again when the plane finally was fully boarded. There were a series of small delays, but eventually they were able to push back from the gate and start the second leg of their journey.

A little over twenty minutes later, they were once again poised at the end of a long runway, prepared to jump into the unknown and plow onward to the east chasing the morning.

Their gigantic 747, now fully loaded with fuel and passengers for the long hop across the Pacific Ocean, took a little longer to become airborne that time, but when it did, the huge machine did so with surprising grace, efficiently carrying them aloft, far above the world below.

Flight attendants offered another snack, but James declined, instead taking a sleeping pill he'd brought with him just for this occasion. Twenty minutes later, his seat was once again fully reclined and he was sound asleep. Patrick again faced a long haul without his brother's company or conversation.

With nothing else to do, Patrick flipped through the entertainment options available. He saw a variety of movies were available to watch, but he recognized none of the actors or stories, so instead of entertaining and distracting him, they only served to further depress him and make him wish he'd never left Jack.

Giving up on entertainment, Patrick felt instead like his entire world was crumbling away. The only world he'd known, the man he loved, had all been taken from him. He regretted his decision a thousand times during that long flight to the United States.

Hour after hour their flight pushed ever eastward. Patrick looked out the window at the sky. There was nothing to see out there. But there was nothing inside for him to see either.

Desperate finally for some distraction, Patrick put on the headphones supplied by the flight attendant and watched a sitcom. It was meant to entertain and to amuse. A lot of it went over his head, but at the same time some elements of it did distract him from his self-torment about leaving Jack.

After sleeping for about seven hours, James awoke and raised his seat back upright once again. Trying to scrub the remaining sleep from his eyes, he got up and used the restroom, immediately returning to his seat and strapping in again.

"Are we there yet?" James asked with a fake smile.

"No."

"How long?"

"Since we left Hong Kong, we've been flying for about eight hours so far," Patrick answered. "So that means we've got about five hours left to go."

James groaned in obvious distaste of the answer Patrick had just given.

"But when I was up walking around once, I spoke with one of the flight attendants. He was very friendly and talkative. He said we've had a fantastic tail wind so far and we're making incredibly good time, so perhaps it will be less."

The tail wind that had helped them continued, and four hours and thirty minutes later they were on final approach into Los Angeles International Airport. When their plane was parked at the gate, James practically leapt from his seat, grabbed his carry-on bags, and briskly ordered, "Come on, let's go."

Patrick didn't share his brother's enthusiasm or his eagerness. He only rose from his seat when he had no choice. He didn't have much with him, so he was able to easily grab the backpack James had bought for him in Thailand and follow James when the time was right.

As they walked down the Jetway, Patrick stopped James with a hand to his arm.

"Are your parents waiting in there for you?"

"Not here. We have to go through all the formalities first. They'll meet us after that."

"Oh, okay," Patrick said, not having a clue what James was talking about with the word "formalities." But he quickly found out as he waited in a long snaking line to submit his form and show his passport. The actual time with the agent was minimal. The wait to get to an agent, however, was long.

James retrieved his checked luggage, and then they were free to exit the restricted area. They were not stopped in customs, so they proceeded directly into a large crowd of people, presumably waiting for someone who had yet to clear the "formalities," as James had called them.

"There they are," James said with a smile, pointing at someone at the back of the crowd. James was so obviously excited, so up, so animated and happy. "Stick with me," he ordered as he stepped briskly through the crowd.

"I'm not letting you out of my sight," Patrick assured him, suddenly consumed with fear at having to deal with new strangers. And that was what they were most likely going to be to him. He knew it. They'd be strangers, just like everyone else had been for months now.

The people James was guiding them toward were older than him and leaned a bit into each other; it was only when he got closer that he saw they were holding hands. The woman was shorter than him, closer to James's height. But the man was his own height. The woman was dressed beautifully, much more so than other women around them. The man wore much the same as he and James did. Her hair was elaborately styled in some way that was foreign to Patrick; maybe it was the style here.

They made their way through the crowd of happy and excited travelers and families, and at last stood before two people Patrick did not recognize. It would probably be more accurate to say James stood in front of those people. Patrick cautiously stood behind James, where he felt a bit safer.

To the best of his knowledge, Patrick had never met them before, and in point of fact, he wasn't especially eager to meet them now. James hugged his mother. Only when he had to did he extend his hand to formally shake hands with the man. This move appeared to startle him, but he recovered quickly and took the hand.

"It's nice to meet you, sir," Patrick said formally, bowing slightly.

The woman who stood beside him would not settle for a handshake. Before he knew what was happening, she had thrown herself at Patrick and had her arms wrapped tightly around him.

"Thank God you're alive and that we've got you back."

Patrick could hear her crying, but she was holding him so tightly he couldn't move his head to see. Patrick didn't know the woman, or couldn't remember her, so he found this very awkward, holding his arms out to his sides so he could be prepared to push her away if he couldn't take it. He was bending forward slightly since she was shorter than he was. He found the whole thing to be entirely too awkward and uncomfortable.

When she finally released him, he looked to James for help.

"This is your mother," James said.

"Oh. It's nice to meet you, ma'am." Patrick repeated his formality with her, despite the earlier hug.

"So it's true," his father said. "You really don't know us."

"I do not know you—either of you. I do not recognize you. I have no idea who you are. To the best of my knowledge, we have never met before."

"I'm your father, son. We've been terribly worried about you. You just disappeared. It was like you fell off the planet."

"Oh. Sorry about that… I guess."

"Now I've got you back here, I'm going to go home to see my wife and my children."

"Okay," Patrick said, preparing to leave with him.

"No, Patrick," James said. "You're going to stay with Mom and Dad."

A panic-stricken look blossomed on his face. "No!" Patrick protested loudly, attracting the attention of many of the travelers around them in the crowded airport terminal. "No! I don't know them. I don't know who they are. You are not going to abandon me with two total strangers. I came here because you asked me to. I did it. You promised me you'd stay with me, but already you're trying to abandon me to people I don't even know. You are not going to just dump me with these strangers. If that's your plan, then you're going to buy a ticket so I can go home, right now." It was impossible to miss the sheer panic in his voice.

"Patrick!" He heard his mother scold. "You're creating a scene. We're your parents. We raised you. Who better to watch over you now? You're home, dear," his mother said.

"No offense, ma'am. You might be a lovely person, but I don't know you. I know *nothing* about you. I don't trust you. And nothing here is what I would call home. The only home I know is the place I left to come here, the place I wish I'd stayed. I never should have left Jack and home."

"We're your parents, son," his father said. "We love you."

"That's nice," Patrick said, refusing to leave James's side. His ramrod-stiff posture alone conveyed his level of discomfort.

"Patrick, it's okay. They won't hurt you. I can't take you home with me. We don't have the room for a guest with the two children. But I'm only about ten minutes away from where you're going to be."

Patrick stared at James. "I do not know them," he said between gritted teeth.

"Patrick. It's okay. They're good people." He pulled out a business card and wrote something on the back, then handed it to Patrick. "This is my cell phone number. If you need anything, just call me. I'm planning to go home and hug my family, but I'll do whatever I can to help. You really are safe with them. They raised us from babies to adulthood. And I'm not going to be all that far away."

Patrick again looked suspiciously at the two people, seeing them smiling hesitantly at him.

No doubt they were as uncomfortable with the way this encounter was going as he was.

Patrick shook his head slowly, looking back at James. "I'm tired, and I want to go home."

"Did you get any sleep on the flight?"

"No," Patrick said through clenched teeth.

"There's your problem. Go home with Mom and Dad and get a good night's sleep, and you'll feel a lot better when you wake up. You'll have major jet lag to deal with—"

"What's that?" Patrick asked, something new to add to his list of fears.

"It just means there is a huge time difference between here and Bangkok. Something like ten, eleven, twelve hours. I don't remember which. It's going to take some time to get reacclimated to the local time."

"I don't want to get acclimated to whatever time it is here. I'm not staying here. I'm going home to Thailand. I never should have let you talk me into this. If you leave me, I'm never going to forgive you. You got me here…. You lied to me."

"Son," his father said, taking a step toward him. "We love you. I know you don't recognize us. I can't imagine what you've been through. We promise to take excellent care of you. You have nothing to fear." And even though his mother did not approve, his father said, "If and when you decide to return to Thailand, you of course are free to do so."

But Patrick was stubbornly not giving an inch. With his arms crossed over his chest, he glared to James.

"It really is okay," James tried again, seeming anxious to move this whole thing along.

The yawn that consumed Patrick made it next to impossible for him to deny he was tired. He was bone weary, and he knew his fatigue was likely a contributing factor to his upset.

"Fine," he growled through gritted teeth. "Do these people know how to reach you?" he demanded, making no attempt to hide his anger.

"Yes, Pat. They're my parents too. They know where I live. They know my telephone numbers. They know how to get hold of me at any hour of the day or night. Are we good?" he asked, looking hopeful.

"No! We're not good, but what choice do I have now? You just remember," he said with every iota of resolve he could summon forth, "that you promised you would get me back home to Thailand after I came here and did this... whatever you want to call it. I wish I'd never come, but I'm here. Just remember you're getting me home. I did what you asked. I'm here. And you're going to get me back. Do not try to weasel yourself out of that. We have a deal. If you do not hold up your end of that deal any better than you're holding this up so far, you will not like what will happen because I will hunt you down and treat you like I would treat a rat—I'd chop its head off with a shovel."

"Son!" Patrick's mother tried to protest, but one glare thrown her way and she immediately shut up.

"Yes, Patrick, we have a deal. But we've barely arrived. Give it a little while, please. Go get some sleep. You'll feel better."

"How long?" he demanded.

"I can't give you an exact time since I don't know what doctors you need to see or when you can get in to see them. You'll need to see... everything. You should see where you live; you should see your friends. You'll want to see your office."

"And we've got several specialist appointments lined up for you," their father tossed in.

PATRICK stood fixed in place watching James walk away. He had a horrible time seeing the only man he knew, even somewhat vaguely—aside from Jack—leave him. But he did leave, and Patrick was left alone with two people who knew him, even though he didn't know them.

"Come on, Patrick," his father said without spooking him. "Let's get home. You must be exhausted from your trip. You'll feel better once you've slept and had something to eat."

Without a word of agreement or disagreement, Patrick shouldered his backpack with his few possessions and grudgingly followed the two people who claimed to be his parents.

He didn't speak until they were in their car.

"Where are you taking me?" he demanded.

"To our house," his mother said.

"And where is that?" he asked through gritted teeth. "Could I walk from there back to here? To this airport?"

"Good Lord, no!" his mother said. "No one walks in LA. It's about fourteen miles from here."

"What does that mean?" Patrick asked, watching every turn they made as they exited the airport grounds and started to slowly make their way home. He was determined to memorize every step involved in getting to wherever they were taking him so he could reverse the process and get himself back to this airport if he had to.

It turned out to not be all that difficult, because their destination was close to the same freeway they took from the airport, making the trip a straight shot.

The house his parents lived in looked huge, at least compared to the little place where he and Jack had lived together so happily for as long as he could remember. Jack. Just the thought of the man made his heart break. Why had he left Jack? He wished he'd stayed back where he belonged. His place was beside Jack, not halfway around the world in some foreign land. It didn't matter that here he looked just like most of the people he saw and back in Thailand he and Jack had been the only two men who looked like they did. Jack was home. They could go anywhere. So long as Jack was there, Patrick would be home.

Not only did everything look different, but the air smelled different. Something familiar was missing when he sniffed the air. The air in Thailand was never clean and frequently looked thick enough to cut, but it was also laced with the smells of cooking and spices that made his mouth water. What he remembered from Thailand was all he knew. Maybe this was what clean air looked and smelled like? He didn't know. He only knew it wasn't what he was used to.

And it only got worse when they entered the house. The house was indeed massive. He and Jack existed in such a small space, but it was all they needed. They hadn't wanted for anything so long as they had each other. But Patrick didn't have Jack, and at the moment Jack was the only one who could comfort him and make him feel safe and loved. These strangers couldn't do that for him. And even if they'd been able to, he wasn't in any place to accept it.

Nothing inside the house was any more familiar or recognizable to him than anything else had been since he and his brother had left Thailand. All the furniture looked wrong compared to what he'd known from his time in Thailand. Everything here was too big, too spread out, too… strange.

"Am I supposed to recognize any of this?" Patrick asked, no longer hostile, but not exactly friendly either.

"Yes, that had been our hope," his father said gently.

"Nothing?" he asked with disappointment evident in his voice.

Picking up on the nonthreatening manner of his father, Patrick said softly, "No. Nothing."

"Your old room is ready for you," his mother said as she headed toward what looked to be a kitchen. "Why don't you go put your things in there?"

"All right," he said.

But when she looked back and saw he hadn't moved, she said, "Well?"

"Yes?" he asked. "Is someone going to show me where that is?" He couldn't help it. He snapped at her from pure frustration. "Am I supposed to just go room to room until I find one I like? Is that how it works?" Patrick was beyond exasperated with these people. Why did they all think he knew these things? Hadn't they heard anything he'd been saying all this time?

"No, son," his father said with a sad smile. "Come. I'll show you where it is."

After a long, hot shower, Patrick lay down on the bed and was asleep within minutes. Meals would have to wait until the next day.

Chapter Nineteen
Medical Tests

AS soon as he woke the next morning, or what his body told him should be morning, Patrick was confused because it wasn't light outside. But he was wide awake, so he got up and got dressed. Since he'd missed dinner the previous evening, and the last airplane meal had been quite some time ago, he was starving.

Even though the house was dark, he felt his way to where he thought the kitchen would be. He'd tried to be quiet so as not to disturb anyone else in the house, but when he walked into something he hadn't expected, knocking it over, he made enough noise to wake the dead.

"What's going on?" his mother sleepily asked, trailing behind his father as they looked around the dark room.

"Patrick?" he said. "Are you all right?"

"Sorry. I knocked something over in the dark. I don't know where anything is in your house yet."

"What are you doing up at this hour, dear?" she asked him.

"It felt like it was time to be awake. Jack and I always get up at the same time every day. Even when it rains, we still wake up at the same time." It only took one glance for him to see his parents didn't have a clue what that meant.

They clearly had heard of Jack from James, but neither of his parents asked him anything or said anything about Jack. Patrick missed Jack more than he could stand. He thought of him as soon as he'd woken a few minutes earlier, remembering how wrong it felt to reach across the bed to where Jack should be only to find his spot empty and cold.

"You don't need to be up, if this is too early for you," Patrick offered. "But I'm starving and need to get something to eat."

His mother directed him to the refrigerator, where she'd placed a plate for him the previous evening, and then his parents returned to bed. The clock said it was two o'clock, even though his body didn't agree. In addition to jet lag, there was the fact that Jack always worked nights in the cannery, which added another wrinkle to his body clock adjustment.

When he checked the plate of food his mother had indicated, what he saw was chicken. He had nothing against chicken; in fact he liked chicken a lot. But he wanted something to go with it. He needed something fresh, something not meat.

After poking around in various cabinets, he found some noodles and a few things he used to make a meal with noodles, Thai fish sauce (or the closest he could get to that), stir fried chicken, and pineapple.

When his parents got up five hours later, his mother said, "You didn't eat what I left for you."

"I ate some of it. I made something I knew. I need some more things to cook with. Do you have a market I can go to today? I need a fish vendor and a produce vendor and probably a spice vendor."

"We can take you to our grocery store," his father said.

"What's that?" he asked, the term meaning nothing to him.

"They should have everything you want or need."

THE grocery store proved to be yet another foreign experience for Patrick. He was accustomed to visiting separate stalls in open-air markets to find what he needed for them to cook each day. It seemed most unusual to have to buy things that were not freshly harvested, but came in cans printed with colorful labels. The labels were nice, but he wanted to see what he was buying. The produce section of the store proved as frustrating because most the things they had he did not recognize. Shopping, like everything else in Los Angeles, was so drastically different than what he was accustomed to.

They took him to what was described to him as his home, but nothing there was familiar. For several hours he slowly walked through the place, looking at individual items, peeking into closets and drawers, even though it felt wrong to be intruding into someone's life in that way.

Before they left, they retrieved several changes of clothes for him. Starting almost immediately after that, his parents took him to see a variety of doctors, who did all sorts of testing. For days on end he was scanned and poked and prodded and scanned again from a different angle. He didn't recognize any of the machines they shoved him into, but they all looked inside his body for what he hoped they wanted to see.

Nothing spoke to him. No memories magically appeared to him. His father took him to see people he was supposed to know, but none of them rang any bells for him either.

His fourth morning there, his father took Patrick to the office where he had worked.

"Look who I found," his father called out as he escorted Patrick into the lobby of the elegant and modern suite of offices where his son had worked for several years. The receptionist hugged him, which made Patrick feel uncomfortable all over again. He clearly made her uncomfortable by calling her "ma'am" when she expected him to call her by name. But Patrick didn't have a clue who she was or what her name might be.

A whole bunch of people shook hands with him or tried to hug him. He tried to give strong body language that said, "Back the fuck off," but not everyone picked up on that, so he finally started just shoving his hand at people when they moved to try to hug him. He didn't want strangers hugging him. He barely wanted to shake hands with them. He didn't recognize any of them, and it felt so very odd for total strangers to want to embrace him.

People he didn't know showed him an office he didn't recognize. They had him sit in a chair he didn't know and that didn't feel right to him. The desk was foreign to him. He didn't recognize anything in the room. When his father guided him back to the car, Patrick had the clear sense everyone inside the office they'd just left was as frustrated as he was.

Welcome to the club. Frustration was Patrick's entire existence since he'd arrived in this strange place.

"Well, that was a waste of time," Patrick muttered.

THE next morning his father took him to see another doctor, who looked at all the scans and blood work performed before giving him a neurological exam.

"So, Doc," his father asked. "Do you know what's going on here?"

"Well, Patrick," he said. "I believe all your memories are still there, just hidden from you. Clearly you suffered some sort of physical trauma at the time of your accident in Bangkok that made it impossible for you to pull up those old memories. It was probably major trauma."

"But they're still there?" his father asked anxiously.

"Oh, yes, I believe they are. Of course there is no test I can run that says conclusively they are or they're not. I'm basing this on my experience with other cases like this one."

"Will he remember things eventually?" his father asked.

"I can't say," the neurologist reported, which was clearly not the answer Patrick's father wanted to hear. "In some cases, over time patients do recover some of their memories. What's happening is that the pathways your brain would normally use to pull up memories of past events have been interrupted for some unknown reason, most likely when you hit your head in the accident. Your brain is having to learn new pathways to get to those old memories."

"And how long will that take?" his father asked.

"I wish I could tell you, but something like that is impossible to predict," the doctor said. "Every case is different, but usually by this point I would have expected to see something, some of your prior memories beginning to make their way back to the surface. I'm concerned so many months have passed and nothing has surfaced yet."

Patrick could understand what the doctor was saying, even if his father seemed not to—or tried not to. The doctor was telling him that he might very well never be able to remember things from before the accident.

That afternoon Patrick went for a long walk by himself. He was lonely and more all alone than he had ever felt before. He was a stranger in a strange land all over again. Everyone in this place looked like him and sounded like him, but they weren't like him. Or more accurately, he wasn't like them.

A couple of rainy days descended on the Los Angeles area, which made long outdoor walks impossible. For those days, Patrick sat and stared out the window. When his parents spoke to him, he gave minimal responses, but for the most part he simply sat quietly by himself, missing Jack and home. He just wanted to go home, but his parents were not finished trying to force him to remember things yet.

Day after day they took him from person to person they hoped he'd recognize, and when those didn't work, they took him to a whole host of places they said he had always loved. They took him back to his apartment, but nothing there was remotely memorable or familiar to him.

When the weather cooperated, he took increasingly longer walks on the beach, working up to running. He spent longer and longer stretches running each day, desperate for something to do to wear himself out and fill the time until they'd admit defeat and let him return home.

And every day he missed Jack. Every day he saw something he wanted to point out to Jack, something he wanted to show Jack to get his opinion. But Jack wasn't there, and that just felt wrong. Patrick wanted Jack. He'd always known Jack, and the fact that Jack was missing now felt awful to him. He knew where Jack was, but he kept all those thoughts to himself.

And he desperately missed the touch of Jack's hands on his body, Jack's lips kissing him, Jack caressing him, making love to him. He simply craved Jack, but he did not speak of those things to his parents. Those were his private thoughts, and while his parents seemed desperate to get him to share what he could remember with strange doctors, he didn't share Jack with them—the memories of Jack kept him going through those long, lonely days.

In the back of his mind, he'd decided to give these people one month. He'd made a deal with himself that if, within one month from the time he left home to come to this strange place, he hadn't remembered anything, he would go home. He hadn't shared this with anyone until a few days ahead of that deadline when James joined them for dinner one evening.

Pulling his brother aside, he said, "James, I want to go home. It's nearly been a month now. Nothing has happened, and nothing is going to happen. I've done everything you people have wanted and nothing has changed. I want to go home. I desperately miss home. I need you to buy my plane ticket and get me onto a plane to go home."

James sighed and looked down for the longest time.

Feeling close to panic at his brother's silence and lack of eye contact, Patrick growled, "We had a deal." His anger was obvious, even though he was fighting desperately to keep it mostly contained. "You told me I could go home. I've come here, I've done everything everyone asked me to do, nothing has changed, and now I want to go home."

"Pat, please give it just a little bit longer. I know that's not what you want to hear, but please try to do this. Mom and Dad aren't ready to let you go just yet."

"Are you telling me that they intend to hold me captive here?" Patrick practically shouted at his brother, furious at what was shaping up to be the most catastrophic betrayal of his life if it was true.

"No! Of course not."

"Then I want to go home. I came here like you asked. If they want to see me, they can fly to where I live and see me there, just like you did."

"Please, Pat. Dad is gonna tell you tonight that he wants to take you to New York to see a new team of neurologists to see what they have to say."

"Are they any better than all the doctors I've seen here?" he demanded of his brother.

"I don't know. Mom and Dad hope they are, that they can find out what's going on inside your head. Please," James practically begged. "Just give it a little bit longer."

Patrick glared at his brother with open hostility. "You've told me what they get out of my suffering. But what do I get for everything I'm sacrificing? Huh?"

"What do you do when you go out each day?" James asked, which told Patrick that his parents and James talked outside of his hearing. He wondered what else they had to say about him.

"I run. I'm trying to wear myself out so I don't hurt as much."

"Are you in physical pain?" James asked, looking alarmed.

"I miss Jack. I miss him so much it hurts, and I want to go home to see him. I belong there, with him."

"Have you called him?" James asked.

"I can't. He doesn't have a phone. A couple of our neighbors do, but they always said international calls cost too much to take or to make. It's not like you people do here where you just pick up a phone and call anyone."

Patrick and James were quiet for a moment, each studying the other while trying to not show what they were doing.

"I want to go home," Patrick reiterated.

"Please, Pat, just a bit longer."

"I'm not giving you an open-ended agreement on this," Patrick said. "How long do you expect me to let this drag on? Tell me that. I've been away from home for a month already. A month! I'm not going to just keep getting pushed back. I want to go home, and if you won't help me or at least give me a timeline, then I'll just have to find out how to do it on my own. I don't know what it costs, but you told me I have some money. Everyone here seems so much richer than people in Thailand. Do I have enough to buy a ticket? If not, I'll go do something to start earning some money and then buy a ticket on my own and leave."

"You don't have to do that. You have money."

"Where? How do I get to it? Tell me."

"You have a checking account, a money market account, and investment accounts."

"You make it sound like I'm rich. Do I have enough?"

"Yes, more than enough," James assured him.

"How do I get to that money? I want to use it to go home. Help me do it, please."

"You've been here a month. Give it one more month."

"Another whole month?" Patrick demanded loudly. "No! That's like another lifetime in prison. And that's what this place is to me. I'm in prison. I can't last that long here. I hate it here. And that woman," he said, shaking his hand vaguely toward one of the doors. "She's constantly crowding me, asking me how I'm feeling, what I'm doing, what I'm thinking. And she's always trying to hug me and talk to me. But I don't know her."

"She is your mother, Patrick."

"Fine. She knows that. You know that. But I don't know that. I don't know any of this place or these people. Everyone and everything here is completely foreign to me. I want to go home."

James sighed and glanced downward.

"I do understand," James said softly, taking hold of Patrick's hand for a moment. "But if at all possible, give it one more month, and then we can call it quits. One more month. If nothing happens in one more month, just thirty days, then we pretty much know nothing is going to change."

"And you'll let me go home?" Patrick asked warily.

"I'll help you go home. I'll get you home, like I promised I would."

"But not now," Patrick said morosely.

"I would, but I really, really hope you can tough it out for just thirty more days. I know you're bored as shit. Let's see what we can do to fix that during that time."

Patrick slumped back onto a chair behind him, rubbing his hands over his face, clearly thinking.

"I'll give you two weeks," he finally said. "I'll try. But when day fifteen hits, I'm out of here. Not day sixteen. Day fifteen. Not day seventeen. I'm leaving here on day fifteen. Fifteen days from now. Get out your calendar and mark it in bold red letters, because I'm out of here that day. The countdown begins right now."

Together they agreed upon a date, and James circled it on his calendar.

"Buy the plane ticket," Patrick ordered. "Do whatever you need to do, but I want to have that piece of paper to hold in my hands, showing me that you people are not going to hold me prisoner here."

"I can have my secretary—"

"Do it now!" Patrick ordered sharply.

"I'm not sure I know how. Let me call my office."

James called someone and talked for several minutes. Or rather he talked and then listened for extended periods of time, making one- or two-word answers that punctuated the silence.

"Okay," James said when he disconnected the call. "Your ticket has been purchased. My secretary is printing it all out. I'll pick it up and bring it over to you tomorrow when I come by after work. Is that okay?"

AS James had said earlier, that evening over dinner, their father announced he wanted to take Patrick to New York City to see some new neurologists.

"What's New York City?" Patrick asked. "Is it close? Do we get there by car?"

"No," his mother said. "It's about 2,500 miles away. It takes about five hours to fly there."

"Fine. Whatever," Patrick said. "I've been poked and prodded and scanned every which way already, but if it will make you happy, fine, let's go. When can we do it and get it over with?" he asked through gritted teeth. He profoundly hated having so many strangers touching him. All of them had examined him from top to bottom, but none of them had done a single thing to change who he was or what he knew.

"I'll go call my assistant right now and have him start to set up the medical appointments and get us booked on a flight." Patrick kept forgetting his father worked full-time, since Patrick left the house and spent as much time as possible running or just walking, doing anything except remaining in the house.

AND that was how, two days later, Patrick and his father were up very early and he was on yet another airplane, traveling again to a place he did not know. The only difference was this time his travel companion was his father, and instead of flying back to Jack in Thailand, Patrick was flying farther away from him.

His father didn't crowd him like his mother did. Patrick almost liked his father. He would have liked him if he hadn't been so suspicious of all these strangers. Unlike James, his father remained awake throughout the entire flight. They talked a couple of times about random stuff. Patrick was more relaxed with this stranger than he was with just about all the others. He didn't feel as threatened by his father. Their conversations were almost enjoyable to Patrick.

Patrick watched out the window of the airplane as they flew on hour after hour. This country over which they traveled was so vast.

"Is this all one country?" he asked his father after an hour in the air.

"Yes. It's all the United States. Our country is huge. And so very different from coast to coast."

Patrick nodded silently in agreement. The country was like so many other things—large.

When they landed in New York, Patrick was overwhelmed by the traffic, by so many people all trying to get somewhere different at the same time. There were so many people, so much noise.

The hotel at which their cab dropped them was like everything else—huge. It looked grand. The arching white marble façade, accented with black glass, extended up into the air for who knew how far. And the inside was no less luxurious.

Patrick had thought the Sheraton hotel in Bangkok had been luxurious, but that one had nothing on this one. They had separate bedrooms that shared a common living and dining area. Their room even had a full kitchen, not that either of them cooked.

Since it had taken all day to fly from the West Coast to the East Coast, they did little upon arriving other than eat and go to bed.

The next morning they started a weeklong round of doctor and clinic visits. Even though he'd been poked and prodded and scanned in countless ways, these doctors did the same things all over again. Every morning, the first thing they did was to go see another whole set of doctors who didn't seem to trust anything others had done and insisted on doing the same things over again themselves.

There was one new test this time. One of the hospitals this time attached dozens and dozens of electrodes to his head—so many his entire scalp was covered. Then they spent hours monitoring him, periodically showing him photos projected onto a wall. From the photos James had shown him in Bangkok, he knew these must be family photos, but try as he might, nothing triggered anything. By the end of that morning he wanted to rip the things off his head and start walking back to Bangkok. But he remained still and did what he was asked to do.

Every afternoon they went out and did something touristy. His father had a long list of things he wanted to take his son to do. They rode the ferry boat to the Statue of Liberty.

"Do you recognize her?" his father asked with a huge grin on his face as their boat chugged along toward the huge monument.

"No," he said honestly.

"I brought you here the first time when you were eight years old. You loved this one above all else."

They visited museums, libraries, parks, points at which massive traffic converged. But none of them meant anything special to him. Patrick desperately wished they did, that something did. His father wasn't the only frustrated person on the trip. The only difference was that Patrick kept his frustration to himself.

While there, one night his father took him to a Broadway play. The story meant nothing to him, but the music was glorious. The music sang to him, even though it didn't tell him anything. Somehow, though, it comforted him and made him happy.

BACK in Los Angeles, Patrick quietly kept his countdown. He crossed out days on the calendar he had hung on the back of his bedroom door. Every evening before going to bed, he boldly marked off another day, each one getting him closer to the date circled in red.

Every day he ran mile after mile, trying to tire himself enough that he could sleep. He walked every street he could reach on foot in the city of Los Angeles.

"Where do you go each day?" his mother had asked him one night when he got back to her house.

"I run each morning, and then I walk city streets, looking at people and places."

When he described some of the places he had walked, his mother got quite agitated.

"Oh, no, don't walk there!" she said when he described one area he'd explored just that day. "It's not safe for you to be anywhere near that part of town."

"I've been all over that area. It's very quiet, actually."

"No, Patrick!" she insisted with great urgency. "Please, please, please don't go there. It's just not safe."

"Fine," he said, since the place she was so agitated about meant nothing to him. "I'll find some other part of town to walk."

"Please be careful while you're out there. I worry about you every time you leave the house."

"You shouldn't. I'm fine."

"I do. I'm your mother and that's my job."

Patrick understood her a bit better that evening.

WHEN day fourteen on the timetable he and James had worked out arrived, Patrick called the airline he and

James had flown from Bangkok and asked to confirm his flight to Bangkok the next day was scheduled to leave on time.

Patrick had thought he'd been alone when he made that call, but his mother walked into the room just as he was confirming the flight details.

"What are you doing?" she demanded.

"Confirming my flight for tomorrow."

"What flight?" she pressed him.

"My flight home," he answered directly.

"No!" she shrieked at him, which made him jump back in fear. "You cannot. You will not. I forbid it. You are staying right here where you belong."

"I'm going home. James told me I was free to leave. We have a deal, and that deal is that I go home tomorrow."

"I'm calling him right now," she told him, clearly angry.

"Do anything you want, but I'm going home tomorrow."

AND that led to a full-blown family meeting that left no one happy. Patrick was adamant he was going home. Both of his parents objected, as he knew they would.

"James, you've been quiet," their father said at one point when it appeared his parents had exhausted their arguments. "What do you think about all this?"

"I think Patrick wants to go back to Thailand, and I think that's fine."

"What?" his mother yelled at him. "He's not going anywhere. He's staying right here where he belongs, not halfway around the world, living in squalor where we can't find him. You are to do nothing to help facilitate this crazy idea of his," she ordered.

Patrick looked at his brother, half consumed with anger and half consumed by fear that James wasn't going to honor the deal he'd made with Patrick.

"He wants to go home," James said.

"But he is home!" their mother protested loudly and strongly.

"No, I'm not. I don't know you. I don't know any of this. It's all as much of a mystery to me as it was the day I first arrived here a month and a half ago. I'm frustrated, and I want to go home."

Surprising everyone, James said, "He wants to go home, and that's what we're going to do. I made a deal with him, and I intend to honor that deal, Pat. I'm going with you tomorrow—I'll take you back to Thailand."

"You don't need to," Patrick told him. "Just get me to the airport, and I'll figure it out somehow."

"I know. And you would. I have absolutely no doubt about that. But I'll go with you to make it easier for you, so you can get back without any extra grief or hassle."

And that was how Patrick and James came to spend their next day on another long transpacific flight.

Chapter Twenty
Home?

"AHHHH," James said tiredly as he fell back onto one of the two big comfortable beds in their room, beyond exhausted. "I never want to get on another airplane ever again as long as I live. Seventeen hours in the air is inhumane treatment of the human body and should be declared to be torture."

Patrick snickered. "Not a lot of fun, I'll grant you that. Think what it would have been like if we'd flown coach. Be glad your family has enough money to afford first-class seats."

"It's not my family, Pat. It's *our* family," he gently corrected.

They had checked into their large suite at the Royal Orchid Sheraton Hotel on the banks of the Chao Phraya River in downtown Bangkok, where James had stayed before. Patrick had wanted to go directly to Jack's house, but he knew Jack worked nights and wouldn't be home. Also, there was no place for James at Jack's house, and he didn't feel he could just abandon James after the man had gone to all the trouble of accompanying him all the way from the United States to Thailand.

"I don't know how you used to make that trip several times each year. You… I just don't understand."

"Can't help you there," Patrick agreed, since he had no memory of ever taking the flight until James took him to the United States and now back to the land he knew as home.

"Still nothing coming back to you?" James asked.

"Nope. Not a thing. Just like it's been with everything else. It doesn't matter if people tell me I should know something; I'm just getting nothing. It's like a huge part of my life is just… blank… empty. My life, as I know it, didn't begin until I got here to Bangkok earlier this year."

James had not been wild about the idea of letting Patrick go off to Thailand alone again. Rather than leave anything to chance, he'd had his executive assistant make arrangements for as much of their trip as possible ahead of time, including reserving a car and a professional driver to whisk them from the airport into the city center. There was no way he was leaving their lives in the hands of any cabdriver.

"I'm going to take a shower. Pull me out in about a week or so," James told Patrick as he headed toward the bathroom.

"Okay," Patrick readily agreed.

The window of their hotel room might have shown it was the dark of night—midnight, actually—but Patrick's body did not feel ready to sleep. Sure, the trip had been boring as hell and exhausting, but his entire being was wrapped too tightly to relax. Jack was close. He was so close to Jack, and he couldn't wait to go see him.

Patrick knew James would never agree to going out anywhere so late at night, so his plan was to get his brother into bed and then head out to go find Jack. He thought he could make his way back to the cannery without too much difficulty. In the months he'd lived with Jack, Patrick had become quite skilled at navigating the city.

As he'd hoped, when James came out of the shower, he immediately slid into one of the two beds.

"Night," he told Patrick before closing his eyes and falling asleep. A couple of sleeping pills helped James make the transition quickly.

Patrick stopped in the bathroom to wash his face and use a washcloth to wipe down his arms and his neck before checking James again. Satisfied his brother was out, Patrick headed down to the lobby and asked a bellman to get him a cab to take him to the pineapple cannery. Like James, he'd picked up some local currency before leaving the airport.

And that was when things started to go very wrong.

"No, no," the smaller man said, waving his hands, when he heard where Patrick wanted to go.

"Yes, that's where I want to go. I have a friend there," Patrick emphasized.

"No. No go there. All gone."

"What?" Patrick asked breathlessly.

The bellman gestured for another person in a hotel uniform, someone with a better command of English, to come join them. After a quick conversation in Thai, the new person explained, "I understand you wanted to go see a friend near the old pineapple cannery. You should not go there."

"But I want to go see a friend there," Patrick tried to explain.

"No. Unfortunately, about a month ago, there was a horrific fire in that part of town that destroyed the entire factory and much of the surrounding area."

Patrick gasped. "No! What about the houses the employees lived in on the grounds nearby?"

"All gone. The fire was massive and swept away everything within a quarter mile. It started in a neighboring abandoned warehouse and spread rapidly. We hadn't had much rain when the fire hit, so everything was dry. Once the fire started, it swept uncontrolled through the entire area, including the cannery and all the structures anywhere near there. All the buildings around there were old and constructed of wood. They went up in flames very fast."

"No!" Patrick cried out. "What about the people there? Was anyone hurt?"

"Yes, sadly a great many of the residents were killed in the fire."

"What about those that survived?"

"I don't know, sir. That was weeks ago. They could be anywhere by now."

"But... didn't the factory rebuild?"

"No. They went out of business. The factory was very old and had been there for decades."

"Is there anything there now?"

"No. Just empty lots. I'm sure someone will build there, but nothing has happened yet."

"I need a cab to go there."

"Please, no," the hotel employee implored Patrick. "It would be better to go during the light of the day."

"I know, but... I need... I need to go see for myself."

"Very well. I will tell the cabdriver to wait there for you, though. Otherwise you'll be trapped there with no way to get back. It's a very desolate area now."

"Yes, thank you," Patrick said somewhat absently.

When he'd taken the elevator down, he'd been so full of hope and anticipation to see Jack again. But now? Now he felt like he'd gone through a street fight with a bully and had been not just punched down but pummeled and kicked and stomped on.

He couldn't believe Jack was dead. Jack couldn't be dead. He loved Jack, and he needed Jack. His whole world was wrapped up in Jack. He... he never should have left. He should have been with Jack. His place was by Jack's side, and he'd failed him.

Had he been able to focus on anything other than his anguish, Patrick would have noticed how quickly they covered the distance to the former factory. One advantage of going anywhere at one o'clock in the morning in Bangkok was the traffic was less—not gone, by any means, but definitely less.

As his cab slowed to exit the freeway, Patrick could already see differences in the area. The closer they got to the factory, or what had once been the factory grounds, it was devastating for Patrick. Instead of seeing familiar buildings and finding the little camp where he'd lived with Jack, all he saw was scarred landscape and charred trees that remained standing—at least skeletons of those trees.

Instead of the thriving little community he remembered, all that was left was flat land and scattered piles of debris. It was just empty. Rather than smell the sweet scent of fresh pineapple, all Patrick smelled now was burned wood.

A fence had been erected around the grounds that had once housed the cannery, but Patrick could tell it wasn't a very strong fence and he would be able to get onto the grounds. But it was a very dark night, and he didn't have a flashlight or anything to help him find his way past the ruins to where he'd once lived. He couldn't make that trek now, but he'd come back in the daylight hours and look. He'd explore everything then and try to find someone who had lived there, a survivor of the fire. There had to be someone still around, and if it took him months, he'd find that person and ask them if they knew Jack and if they knew where he'd gone.

Gripping the fence, Patrick felt the tears he'd been holding back escape. He didn't have it in him to fight them any longer.

"Jack!" Patrick screamed at the top of his lungs, his call a sad, mournful cry. He hadn't expected a response, and he didn't get one.

He wept quietly for the loss of fully 50 percent of the life he'd known. Until James had taken him back to the United States, his time in Bangkok was the only life he'd ever known. The people who had lived here had been his people, his friends, his lover. He let the tears fall until there weren't any more left.

Wiping his eyes, he returned to the cab and rode back to the hotel, where he dejectedly made his way back to his room. The shower he should have taken earlier felt good now, but it wasn't enough to wash away his grief. While his brother slept on, Patrick slipped between the crisp, clean sheets on his bed and tried to get some sleep.

Chapter Twenty-One
Burned-Out Remains of a Life

BY the time James woke the next morning, Patrick was sitting slumped in a chair facing the large window of their room overlooking the city far below, his attempt at sleep abandoned.

"You're up already," James said.

"Never went to sleep," Patrick replied, his voice flat, emotionless.

"Sorry, Pat. I wish you could have. I feel worlds better now."

"Good." Patrick hadn't turned around while he spoke.

Apparently something in his tone of voice or posture alerted James to a problem.

"What's wrong?" he gently asked.

"They're all gone," Patrick said, his voice a monotone, devoid of any emotion or animation, devoid of life.

"Who's gone? From where?" James asked.

Patrick knew his brother wouldn't be happy when he heard about Patrick's late-night venture, but he didn't care any longer.

"The factory, all the houses nearby. They're all gone."

"What happened?" James pushed. "And how do you know this to be true?"

"I had a long talk with someone downstairs after you went to sleep." He recounted for his brother the story of the fire as it had been told to him.

"So what do you want to do now?" James asked him.

"Go back now that it's daylight and search."

"Okay, I guess. Wait. What do you mean 'go back'?" James asked.

"I went there last night, but it was too dark to see anything."

"Patrick!" He spoke sharply to his brother. "Don't do that! You cannot go off by yourself. Please! Remember what happened the last time."

"That's just it," Patrick snapped at him. "You remember what happened last time, but I can't. It's your life, not mine. Mine is here. And I've got to go search for Jack, for any of the survivors of the fire."

"Let me take a shower and get dressed. We'll go downstairs and have a good breakfast, and then we'll get our driver to take us over there. But if the area is destroyed, like you described, I don't know what we can possibly do. This might be a shorter trip than we had originally planned."

"Maybe for you, but not for me," Patrick angrily snapped at his brother.

Since he'd showered when he got back the night before, Patrick let James take the bathroom to get ready. Other than basic navigation conversation, the two were silent as they left their room and made their way downstairs in search of food.

Even though he had no appetite, Patrick ate along with James to keep his brother happy. What he really wanted more than anything else was to get into a cab and get the hell out of there and over to where he'd lived so he could search for any clues to where everyone had gone.

He needed to get out of there, and if James didn't finish soon, Patrick was going to bolt and just leave, whether it made his brother happy or not.

Fortunately, though, James seemed to sense what was going on with Patrick and signed the charge for breakfast to their room.

"Okay, let's go back upstairs, grab a few things, and then go."

"Finally," Patrick muttered.

James made a quick phone call, and by the time they were back downstairs, each carrying a backpack with bottled water, a camera, and a few other things, their driver from the previous night was standing in front of the hotel waiting for them. When he spotted the brothers, he bowed slightly, smiled, and held the car door open for them.

But when Patrick explained where they needed to go, the driver clearly didn't know that area and expressed some hesitation.

"Don't worry," Patrick said. "I'll guide you." This earned him a questioning look from the driver. "I lived there for months."

Traffic was as horrendous as usual, so the trip that he'd made quickly the night before now took more than twice as long during the daytime, but finally they did make it.

In daylight the area was stark, devastated. The fire that had swept through must have been unbelievably intense and spread rapidly through all the dry structures.

Where the factory had once stood, there was now only a pile of charred debris, some bricks, burnt beams, and tons of fire-blackened wood and ash. When Patrick started to climb the fence, James grabbed him and said, "Where the hell do you think you're going?"

"In there. I need to see. I need to look."

"Pat, it's not safe."

"I need to see."

And for the next hour, that was what he did. Patrick walked immediately to where he and Jack had once lived, instinctively knowing exactly where the little house they'd shared had been located. He knew he was at the right place when he spotted the water-collecting apparatus Jack had on the roof of his little house. It too was clearly burned, even a bit warped from the high temperatures of the fire, but it was Jack's—there was no question in Patrick's mind.

Using his feet, he pushed aside debris around there, looking for anything. He hoped he didn't find bones, a skeleton. But of course, there wouldn't be anything like that. Thai authorities would have removed bodies long ago. He'd have to find where they went and search for graves.

Clearly lots of people had been over the ground on which he stood. There were untold numbers of footprints in the dirt and the charred remains. Presumably rescuers or investigators. Patrick didn't know how that worked in Thailand, but he would find out.

From the remains of Jack's little house, he found one or two items he recognized, things that had somehow survived the fire. They were small, so he had no trouble pulling them loose and shoving them safely into one of his pockets to take with him.

Devastated by what he was seeing, horrified by the unimaginable loss of life, Patrick felt his tears return. And he let them come. This wasn't just a fire scene; this was his life. He was looking at the remains of his life. No one should have to lose their life twice, but that was how he felt that morning.

What he had back in the United States wasn't his life. This place, here, this was his life. This was what he'd known first and… this was where he'd found love. And now it was where he'd also lost love. It was as if he'd been born here, and now it felt like he was dying here because the life he'd been born into was suddenly ripped away from him.

Patrick felt so fucking angry. He wanted to hit something. He wanted to kick something. He needed some way to get the anger out. He was furious he'd ever let James take him away. If he'd just remained here where he belonged, Patrick could have maybe saved Jack, maybe others. But he hadn't been here. He'd abandoned the one man, the only man, he'd ever loved. And look what that did. Everything was gone. Nothing he'd known remained.

Nearby Patrick spotted a sink from another of the houses that had stood in the area. Still overloaded with anger, he reached out, grabbed the sink, hoisted it aloft, and flung it absolutely as far as he could, screaming in anger. He wanted to throw more stuff. He had to get the anger out or it was going to consume him slowly from the inside.

He found a large rock, which he grabbed, and like a baseball player readying for a pitch, he threw that as far as his arm could hurl it. Several additional things followed until he was panting, gasping for breath.

"Pat?" he heard James ask from close behind him.

Turning toward him, Patrick asked the logical question, "How the hell did you get in here?"

"The same way you did."

"Really? Wish I'd seen that," Patrick said with a hint of a smile.

"You will when we leave, because that's the only way out that I've been able to find. Are you okay?"

"No," Patrick said softly. "No, I'm very much not okay."

"What was this place?" James asked.

"This was where we lived," Patrick explained, speaking softly and still panting to get his breath.

"Really? It looks like it was more… I don't know, industrial, I guess."

"The workers at the cannery had little houses here on the grounds of the main cannery building. They were small, and there were a lot of them."

"And this is where you lived… all those months."

"Yes," Patrick said, finally able to breathe normally again, and now somewhat more in control of his emotions. "That is, after the first week, when Jack was able to bribe me to come out of where I was hiding."

"You were hiding?" James asked. "Right. I guess I forgot you told me about that."

"I didn't know where I was. I didn't know who I was. I didn't know anything. I was beyond confused, beyond terrified. I hid. And at night when trucks came in filled with pineapples, fresh from the field, I'd dash out the best I could with my injuries and grab the pineapples that fell off the trucks and take them back to my hiding place."

"My God," James said, a look of horror on his face.

"I thought I was so slick, but I guess I wasn't. People saw me. They told Jack, since he was a white guy like me. He tried to get me to come out, but I pretended to hide so he wouldn't see me. He was a persistent fucker, though. He came back, brought water, food, toilet paper. The man kept me alive.

"Eventually I came out and talked to him through the fence. I learned I could trust him. He took me in, cleaned me up, gave me some clothes. He took care of me, fed me, helped me get back to wellness. I owe him everything. I should have been here with him. I'm alive because of him, and I abandoned him when he needed me."

They stood in silence for several moments before James asked a question Patrick didn't anticipate. "Where did you hide?"

Patrick looked up and immediately pointed to the spot where he'd hidden. Surprisingly, it looked relatively undamaged.

"Show me," James said, so Patrick started to lead him toward it. When they got there, Patrick saw something that caught his eye. He slid under the old fence and made his way to where he'd hidden.

"Oh my God!" he shouted. Patrick screamed for joy, the sound unintelligible but clearly one of excitement and happiness. "Jack's alive! He left me a note. He's alive! Hallelujah!"

"What? How?" James asked. As much as he appeared to hate getting dirty, James followed the same route Patrick

had taken and joined him. He found Patrick holding a
written note sealed in a plastic bag with his name written
on one side in big red letters.

"Open it," James urged.

But Patrick's hands were shaking. "I can't. Can you?"

"Sure." James took the letter from him and
removed it carefully from where it had resided for who
knew how long.

> *Dear Patrick,*
> *Sorry I'm not here to greet you
> like I promised. As you can see, we
> had a bit of excitement here while
> you were gone. We lost a lot of
> good people, mostly older folks who
> couldn't run or who were overcome
> by the smoke. I got as many out as I
> could, but it got so hot so fast, and
> there was so much smoke, I couldn't
> get more. That hurt so bad, knowing
> there were still people in there,
> trapped and dying just yards from
> where I stood. But the fire pushed
> us back. The police questioned
> everybody. They were suspicious
> of me and asked for identification.
> Obviously I didn't have any, but they
> were not satisfied. They're deporting
> me back to Australia. I don't know
> what I'll do there. It's been so long
> since I've been "home." They weren't
> wild about me when I left; I can't
> imagine they'll welcome me with open
> arms now. But I guess I'll find out. I*

know it's unlikely, but if you find this note, I'm going to be in Port Douglas, Australia. That's on the eastern coast, north of Brisbane. Ask for Jack Williams and maybe you'll find me. Please take care and have a wonderful life, my special friend. I will always love you. Never forget that.
    Jack

Patrick was crying again, but this time with joy.

"I'm going to Australia," he said, immediately heading back toward the fence. He scaled it in three easy steps.

"Wait for me," James shouted after him. "Patrick, I can't get over that fence without your help."

They finally did get him over the fence and back into the car. After a trip back into town to shower and change clothes, they were back in the car for an unexpected return trip to the airport and a Qantas flight to Brisbane with a stop and change of planes in Sydney.

As they started down the Jetway toward their flight, James groaned, "Ugh. More time in a plane. What fun."

Chapter Twenty-Two
On the Road Again

THEIR flight from Bangkok to Sydney wasn't as long as the marathon flight they'd had across the Pacific, but it was nearly ten hours. James called it ten hours, saying, "Nine hours and fifty-one minutes is ten hours in plane time."

They'd been lucky to find two first-class seats on the flight at the last minute. Patrick hadn't told James, but he would have been on the flight even if he'd had to sit in the middle of a crowded row deep in coach. Fortunately, though, it didn't come to that. Patrick couldn't imagine what James would have said in a situation like that, and he was glad he didn't have to find out.

"Have you ever been to Sydney?" Patrick asked as they deplaned and waited for their connecting flight, which was thankfully only an hour. It felt good to be up and walking around after ten hours in the air.

"Are you kidding me? Hello, I'm the guy who didn't ever want to leave home. I didn't want to go anywhere. I'm like Mom in that regard. If it worked for her, it worked just fine for me as well," James said.

When boarding for their next flight was called, they queued up and made their way on board. James again groaned, but Patrick was practically bouncing with excitement.

Once they were airborne, James, ever the logical one it seemed, asked an important question.

"Okay, once we get there, what the hell are we going to do? What's your plan?"

"Find Jack."

"Okay, does that mean stand on the street corner by the airport and clap your hands while calling his name? Like someone would call a dog to come inside?"

"Don't be silly," Patrick scoffed.

When a flight attendant passed through, offering beverages, James asked an all-important question. "Do you know if Port Douglas is a long distance from where we'll be landing?"

"About a half hour's driving time, as I recall, love," she told him.

"Thank you," he said with a smile. Turning back to Patrick, he said, "Don't they drive on the wrong side of the street in Australia?"

"How would I know?" Patrick asked, obviously frustrated by the question.

"Because you've been to Australia about a dozen times, as I recall. This and Thailand were two of your frequent travel sites."

Patrick was silent. He so desperately wished he could remember. Now more than ever, he wanted to remember. He closed his eyes and tried so hard to find his missing memories. He tried to picture what he'd heard or read about Brisbane and Australia and Sydney. But nothing. He squeezed his eyes shut, grabbed the armrests tightly, leaned forward, and tried so very hard for anything, a glimmer of a memory, a single thread, a hint—anything.

Patrick felt like there was something there, but no matter what he did, he couldn't reach those memories. "Fuck!" he swore, startling several people around them, as well as his brother.

"What's wrong? Did you remember something?"

"No. It feels like it's there, but I just can't remember."

"Focus on the positive," James told him.

"What's positive?" Patrick asked.

"You know there're memories there. You can feel something there. That's positive."

"Fine. But it would be better if I could remember something."

WHEN their flight landed, Patrick practically ran over anyone who dared to get in his way in a race to get through all the formalities and then to retrieve their bags and find a place to rent a car.

"Now," the clerk at the car rental counter said, "I need to warn all my American customers to be very careful until you get used to driving on our roads. Especially be careful in the roundabouts."

"What's a roundabout?" James asked.

"Traffic circle," the clerk explained.

Five minutes later they were in their car and on their way off the airport grounds and headed north toward Port Douglas. James squealed in fear several times, but Patrick was singly focused on driving and putting as many miles—or kilometers—behind them as possible.

Much to James's surprise, Patrick took to driving on the left side very easily. His father had replaced his driver's license for him back in Los Angeles, not that driving in the US was the same as driving in Australia. Patrick got them to Port Douglas without a single incident. In town, Patrick parked and jumped out of the car, looking all around.

"Now what?" James asked.

"We've got to start asking people if they know him and where I can find him. I'll take everything on that side of the street," Patrick said, indicating the left side of the street, "and you take everything on this side of the street. We'll meet up back here when we're done."

Before James could agree or disagree, Patrick was off, dashing inside the open doors of a bar.

For an hour, they knocked on doors or went into shops and restaurants. The question was always the same. "I'm looking for a man named Jack Williams. He just got back from Thailand. Do you know him? Do you know where I can find him? It's very important."

But over and over again the answer was the same. "Sorry, mate. Never heard of the bloke."

When they met up back at the car a little over an hour later, Patrick looked dejected—more so when he saw the lack of excitement on his brother's face.

"No luck, I take it?" Patrick asked.

"No luck. I asked everyone I could find. I even went one by one to every person in a bar. Can we get a room somewhere and get some sleep? I'm really whipped. We can continue tomorrow when there'll be more people out and about. I'm sure we'll have better luck then."

"I suppose you're right. There's a place just back down the road about ten miles that we passed driving in here. It looked nice from what I could tell. Let's go there."

Since James was beyond exhausted, he readily agreed, and they were back in the car and headed back down the road a couple of minutes later, the prospect of a soft bed and pillow calling to both of them.

When Patrick spotted the sign for Turtle Cove resort on the left-hand side, he slowed and turned in, then parked near where the sign indicated the office was located. Getting a room had been a gamble since there hadn't been a lot of other obvious choices, but it had paid off since the resort had a couple of rooms left.

When they deposited their bags in the room, Patrick asked, "You hungry?" He was hungry and wanted to eat so he could sleep and get back out there to hunt for Jack.

"Starving," James agreed.

"They're still serving dinner here, from what the guy at the front desk said. Let's go eat and then call it a night."

"Deal," James tiredly agreed.

It wasn't difficult to locate the dining area, and they easily got a table and ordered something simple and quick. Dining could come another day. Tonight was simply about feeding.

Patrick had his head down on the table, rubbing a crick in his neck, when someone appeared and needed the table space.

"Sorry, mate," he heard a voice say. "Bread and butter for you before your meals come out."

Patrick's head shot up like a flash. He gasped. That voice! He knew that voice! He started to get a little light-headed before he realized he'd been holding his breath.

"Jack?" he yelled loud enough for people back in Port Douglas to be able to hear him.

He was on his feet now, rising so quickly he knocked his chair backward and onto the floor, creating more of a huge racket in the process.

"Buddy? Er, Patrick?" Jack said excitedly. "Oh my God! It's you. You found me!"

Wasting no time, they threw themselves at one another, Patrick lifting Jack off the floor and spinning him around a little, his arms wrapped tightly around the other man.

"It's you. It's really you. I found you. Jack, I found you."

"You found me. You found me. Put me back down, mate."

"Oh, right, sorry," he said, setting Jack down and grabbing his hands instead. "Jack, I was so scared when I got back to Bangkok and heard about the fire. I searched the entire area where the cannery once stood. I walked to where we lived."

"You must have found my note," Jack said with a smile so big it threatened to break his face into two parts. "How in the world did you find me?" Jack asked. "I don't care—you found me. That's all that matters."

"We went door-to-door in town, searching for you, but we had no luck. We were both beat, so I drove us back here to get a room if they had one. They did… and here you are. And here we are."

Patrick couldn't help himself. He grabbed Jack again, hugging him as tightly as possible.

"I love you, Jack. I love you and I'm never letting you go again. Ever."

"Deal."

And if their words didn't seal the deal, the all-consuming kiss that followed sure would have. Love had conquered tragedy and in the end triumphed in the face of adversity. What more could two men in love ask for? Not a single thing.

Coming in August 2018

Dreamspun Desires #63
The Missing Ingredient by Brian Lancaster

It can take losing everything to realize what you had all along.

Up-and-coming London chef Marcus Vine is poised on the edge of success, but the only men courting him are investors. That leaves Marcus with some free time—which is fortunate, because his godchildren need him.

A year ago, a horrible accident killed Marcus's best friend, Raine, leaving her children without a mother and her husband, Tom, without a partner. Consumed by grief, Tom has been going it alone, refusing help, but when Marcus sees him out with the children, it's obvious that Tom and his two daughters need someone. His persistent caring finally wears Tom down, allowing him to accept the comfort Marcus offers. Soon Marcus is up to his elbows in homework, home-cooked meals, and after-school activities. Over time he helps them rebuild their world, until soon their lives are approaching normal.

Then the unexpected happens: Tom confesses he has romantic feelings for Marcus, and nothing can ever be the same.

Dreamspun Desires #64
Rocking the Cowboy by Skylar M. Cates

Opposites who go together like country and rock and roll.

Long before he was a superstar, Remy Sean had a secret crush on Jed Riley. But Jed sees Remy as a spoiled pop rocker and an extension of his father's control. Still, Jed is willing to let Remy hide from the press on his ranch—but only as a way to get his father out of his life and business for good.

Used to being admired and fawned over, Remy keenly feels the sting of Jed's dismissal. Can he make Jed see him as more than a pain in the ass? Or is Jed too tangled up in his ranch to see past his old hurt?

Jed doesn't believe someone desired by so many fans could want him, a simple cowboy. But Remy is determined to change Jed's mind and steal his heart….

Now Available

Dreamspun Desires #59
His Leading Man by Ashlyn Kane

He wrote a comedy. Fate directed a romance.

Drew Beaumont is bored of the same old roles: action hero, supervillain, romantic lead. He's not going to let a fresh gay buddy comedy languish just because they can't find him the right costar. No, Drew bats his eyelashes and convinces everyone that the movie's writer should play Drew's not-so-straight man.

Aspiring writer Steve Sopol has never had a screenplay optioned. Now one of Hollywood's hottest properties wants to be in a movie Steve hasn't finished writing—and he wants Steve as his costar. Turns out the chemistry between them is undeniable—on and offscreen.

Drew swore off dating in the biz, but Steve is the whole package: sharp, funny, humble, and cute. For Steve, though, giving in to the movie magic means the end of the privacy he cherishes. Will the credits roll before their ride into the sunset?

Dreamspun Desires #60
The Best Worst Honeymoon Ever by Andrew Grey

How can heartbreak turn into happily ever after?

Tommy Gordon is all set for happily ever after—until heartbreak strikes when his husband-to-be leaves him at the altar. In a bid for distraction, his best friend, Grayson Phillips, suggests he takes advantage of the luxury honeymoon anyway! But the last thing Tommy wants is to go alone, so he invites Grayson and his son, Petey, along.

Beautiful Bonaire lends itself to romance, and along with close quarters, relaxing on the water, and a matchmaking kid, Tommy and Grayson soon find themselves closer than ever… and considering more, much to Grayson's delight. But before they can plan the best best honeymoon ever, dark clouds descend in the form of Tommy's ex and a sting from paradise that could ruin everything.